***Ten days, Gray thought.
Lord, he was still shaking! She's going
to be here for another ten days!***

Ten more days of him and Jill rubbing up against each other, the way two people inevitably did when they shared the same space. Ten more days of bumping into her in doorways, of watching the way she ate and the way she laughed and the way she so tenderly kissed and hugged her son.

"This would be a whole lot easier if we weren't married," he muttered aloud in his room.

There was something about being married. He kept thinking about what marriage meant. It meant sharing. Sharing their space, as he was doing with Jill. Sharing their stories. They'd begun to do that, too, the very first night they met. Sharing their lives…

And marriage meant one more thing, too. It meant sharing a bed.

Dear Reader,

Although it will be archived by now, I've been writing to readers on our www.eHarlequin.com community bulletin boards about Silhouette Romance and what makes it so special. Readers like the emotion, the strength of the heroines, the truly heroic nature of the men and a quick, yet satisfying, read. I'm delighted that Silhouette Romance is able to fulfill a few of your fantasies! Be sure to stop by our site. :)

I hope you had a chance to revisit *Lion on the Prowl* by Kasey Michaels when it was out last month in a special collection with Heather Graham's *Lucia in Love*. Be sure not to miss a glimpse into those characters' lives with this month's lively spin-off called *Bachelor on the Prowl*. Elizabeth Harbison gives us *A Pregnant Proposal* from our continuity HAVING THE BOSS'S BABY. Look out next month for *The Makeover Takeover* by Sandra Paul.

Other stories this month include the second title in Lilian Darcy's THE CINDERELLA CONSPIRACY. Be assured that *Saving Cinderella* has the heartwarming emotion and strong heroes that Lilian Darcy delivers every time! And Carol Grace has spun off a title from *Fit for a Sheik*. This month, look for *Taming the Sheik*.

And we've got a Christmas treat to get you in the mood for the holidays. Carolyn Greene has *Her Mistletoe Man* while new-to-the-line author Holly Jacobs asks *Do You Hear What I Hear?*

I hope that you enjoy these stories, and keep in touch.

Mary-Theresa Hussey

Mary-Theresa Hussey,
Senior Editor

Please address questions and book requests to:
Silhouette Reader Service
U.S.: 3010 Walden Ave., P.O. Box 1325, Buffalo, NY 14269
Canadian: P.O. Box 609, Fort Erie, Ont. L2A 5X3

Saving Cinderella

LILIAN DARCY

SILHOUETTE *Romance*®

Published by Silhouette Books

America's Publisher of Contemporary Romance

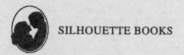

SILHOUETTE BOOKS

ISBN 0-373-19555-9

SAVING CINDERELLA

This edition published by arrangement with Harlequin Books S.A.

Visit Silhouette at www.eHarlequin.com

Printed in U.S.A.

Books by Lilian Darcy

Silhouette Romance

The Baby Bond #1390
Her Sister's Child #1449
Raising Baby Jane #1478
*Cinderella After Midnight #1542
*Saving Cinderella #1555

*The Cinderella Conspiracy

LILIAN DARCY

has written nearly fifty books for Silhouette Romance and Harlequin Mills & Boon Medical Romance (Prescription Romance). Her first book for Silhouette appeared on the Waldenbooks Series Romance Bestsellers list, and she's hoping readers go on responding strongly to her work. Happily married, with four active children and a very patient cat, she enjoys keeping busy and could probably fill several more lifetimes with the things she likes to do—including cooking, gardening, quilting, drawing and traveling. She currently lives in Australia but travels to the United States as often as possible to visit family. She loves to hear from fans, who can e-mail her at darcy@dynamite.com.au.

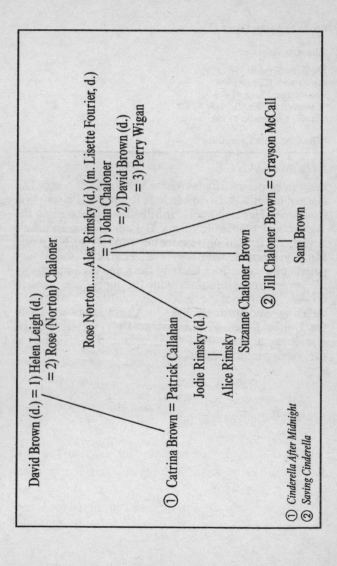

David Brown (d.) = 1) Helen Leigh (d.)
                 = 2) Rose (Norton) Chaloner

Rose Norton.....Alex Rimsky (d.) (m. Lisette Fourier, d.)
                          = 1) John Chaloner
                          = 2) David Brown (d.)
                          = 3) Perry Wigan

① Catrina Brown = Patrick Callahan

Jodie Rimsky (d.)
    |
Alice Rimsky

Suzanne Chaloner Brown

② Jill Chaloner Brown = Grayson McCall

Sam Brown

① *Cinderella After Midnight*
② *Saving Cinderella*

Prologue

Jill didn't even know his name. He was staring down at her with black eyes that swam with the brilliant reflection of the colored lights that surrounded them. The heavy silk folds of her wedding dress brushed against his legs, and he let his hand rest on her bare forearm for a moment.

"Is this okay?" he muttered in a low voice, roughened with a Montana-bred burr.

Jill gave a tiny nod. "Mm."

"You didn't look happy before."

"Much better now."

"Good! I think they're ready for us. Are you sure about this? We could just leave. Tell them to go jump."

"I can't. It's in the contract. I'm filling in for someone, and she'd lose her job if I didn't go through with this."

"Okay." He nodded. "That makes sense. I couldn't see why you'd want to."

"I'm fine," Jill insisted.

But she wasn't. Not really. She was missing her little son horribly. She hated being here in Las Vegas, when he was all the way back home in Philadelphia. She'd skated the role of Cinderella in the ice show tonight, as understudy to the regular lead, who was ill. It was the starring role she'd always wanted, but it came with conditions attached.

TV cameras and strangers staring. A "waiver" and a "license" to sign. An emcee leering at her figure, closely molded and on display inside the gorgeous designer wedding gown. He was calling her "our Celebrity Cinderella Bride" and he'd encouraged the men at this so-called ball to bid for her.

Which they had. Red-faced, over-eager. Drunk, some of them, she suspected.

Not this man, though, the one who had won her at last, for over five hundred dollars. There was something much steadier about this one. His dark eyes, his solid stance, the questions he asked about her well-being. And when they faced each other, ready to enact the charade of their wedding vows, his warm hands held hers steadily, too.

Behind him, the lettering on the huge sign blurred in Jill's vision. "Cinderella Marriage Marathon," it read. "Win the coach, the palace, the honeymoon… and the bride!"

"Ready, you two?" said a man who was dressed like a royal courtier from days gone by, in a wig of rippling white curls, satin breeches and embroidered waistcoat.

For the first time, the audience fell silent. The other couples were ready and waiting now. The emcee launched into a spiel that Jill barely listened to. She caught only a few phrases, and didn't take the time to make sense of them.

"...officer of the court present to witness...progress of each marriage on live cable TV...last couple left standing...winner takes all."

The cameras had moved in closer, stealing her attention, and the lights had gotten even brighter. There was a mirror ball directly above her head, sending tiny white lights chasing across the black-eyed stranger's face. A burst of romantic music vibrated in the air, then died away.

"Do you, Grayson James McCall, take Jillian Anne Chaloner Brown to be your lawfully wedded wife...?"

Grayson McCall. That was his name. She looked up at him. Their eyes met and held.

And even though she knew it was meaningless, a stunt, a charade, she was suddenly captured by the magic and swept away. She could have wrapped herself in the warm light of those eyes like wrapping herself in a black velvet cloak. How would it feel if a man like this was saying words like this to her, not as part of some reality TV gimmick, but for real?

"I do," he said.

His voice was low, and his gaze never left her face for a second. It was a moment she'd never forget.

Chapter One

Sam was getting sick.

Jill had started to suspect it a couple of hours ago, just before the cheap rental car she'd picked up yesterday evening broke down half a mile this side of Blue Rock. Now, sitting with Sam as a passenger in a different vehicle, she was sure of it.

"You didn't finish the story, Mommy," he whined.

Sam never whined. Unless he was getting sick.

Jill felt his forehead—it was hot. "Yes, I did, honey," she soothed him, putting an arm around his little shoulders and pulling him close. The rear seat of the Cadillac was shiny with age. They hit a bump in the dirt road and Sam's hip slid hard against hers.

"No, you didn't," he argued, his voice rising. "You never said the bit about living happily ever after."

Well, he had her there. She never had said it, and everyone knew that all good fairy stories should end that way.

She sighed.

The problem was that the tale she'd been spinning to her son over the past quarter of an hour wasn't a fairy story. It was her makeshift attempt to explain to a four-year-old, fatherless boy why they'd come all the way by train from Pennsylvania to Montana to resolve a situation that she'd never meant to get into at all.

Sam adored trains. He hadn't asked a single question about the reason for this trip during that part of the journey. But then they'd gotten off the train in Trilby. They'd rented a wreck of a car from the cheapest place in town—"affiliated nationwide" its sign had claimed, but she wasn't impressed—spent a sleepless night in a noisy, down-market motel just off Interstate 15, and made it, this morning, as far as Blue Rock.

The car had given up completely about two hours ago, in a hissy fit of noise and ominous smoke. No "happily ever after" involved in this instance. Bored, exhausted and getting sick, Sam had finally asked, "What are we doing this for, anyhow?"

Jill sighed again.

Maybe she shouldn't have tried to make her story so upbeat and reassuring. No wonder Sam wanted the fairy tale ending, when she'd started by talking about the pink colored lights and the silk wedding gown, Cinderella on silver skate blades and a handsome prince in a cowboy's hat who'd swept her away from that nightmare of a ball....

"Looks like this could be Grayson up ahead, there, on horseback," said the balding man at the wheel of the noisy Cadillac. For a car mechanic's vehicle, it didn't sound as though it was in great shape. "I'll pull over."

"I—" Jill began, then stopped.

From the first, she hadn't particularly taken to Ron Thurrell, the owner-operator of Blue Rock's one gas station and vehicle repair shop. He was apparently also the local agent for Triple Star Insurance, as well as for two minor car rental companies.

She *should* have taken to him. He'd gone out of his way with his offer to drive her and Sam the twenty-four remaining miles to Grayson McCall's isolated ranch. He had also promised to deal with the rental car and have another one ready for her when she needed it. He'd definitely been helpful, but she hadn't liked him, and she didn't want to admit to him that Gray had no idea she was coming. Definitely didn't want to admit to him what she was here for.

"Okay. Thanks," she said instead.

Mr. Thurrell slowed the vehicle to a halt and Jill saw the rider on horseback in the distance, heading diagonally in this direction across a field of tall grass. She got out of the car, shut the door to keep the insistent September wind off Sam's flushed little face, and went over to the barbed wire fence that bordered the track.

Leaning on one of the wooden posts, she wondered if there was some special kind of call or gesture people out here used to summon each other across such yawning expanses of land. She wasn't quite sure yet if the rider—was it really Gray?—had seen her. Tentatively, she waved one hand. Then she lifted off her winter wool hat and waved again with that, more forcefully.

Grayson McCall, if it was him, had seen and understood. Jill could see it by the way he quickened the horse's stride. As he approached, she began to get a sense of his ease in the saddle. Knowing nothing whatsoever about horses—she'd seen them in the flesh maybe, oh, twice?—she could still recognize what a capable rider he was.

He held his body in a lazy cowboy slouch, which she could tell was totally comfortable and controlled. He seemed like a knight in shining armor, but that was a comparison she should most definitely steer clear of.

Half a minute later, she knew for certain that it was Grayson. She hadn't seen him since March, almost six months ago, but her memory of him was still surprisingly strong. She hadn't forgotten his big, hard, capable body, and his straight, soft hair. It was the color of black-strap molasses shot through by a shaft of sunlight, and it had felt silky against her fingers. She hadn't forgotten his jutting jaw, with its suggestion of ranch-bred stubbornness, nor his straight, strong nose, steady dark eyes and brown, outdoor skin.

She hadn't forgotten, either, how it had felt when he'd kissed her. Now, that was something that belonged in a fairy tale, for sure!

And now he had recognized her, which must have been more of a challenge. She had let her dark hair grow longer over the past few months. Today it was scraped back in a ponytail which had taken her not more than thirty seconds to fix in place with a bright pink scrunchy some hours ago at the motel.

Last time they'd met, she'd been wearing a perfect mask of makeup and that gorgeous silk wedding gown.

Now she wore blue jeans, a snug pink sweater and pink padded jacket, with no makeup at all.

But he recognized her, all right. He tensed up in the saddle and unconsciously slowed the horse's gait. As he got closer, she could see beneath the battered brown felt cowboy hat to his black eyes. They were courteous and wary at the same time.

Reaching the fence, he reined the horse in and Jill registered the unfamiliar sounds of creaking saddle and clinking bit and stirrups. She saw the way Gray's thighs, clad in old blue denim, moved easily against the leather beneath him. It was as if he and the horse were one.

The large chestnut brown animal whickered impatiently and shifted its hooves. Maybe it knew this wasn't the place it and its rider were supposed to end up. It smelled pungently of oats and farmyard.

"Hello, Jill," Gray said in his gruff voice.

"Hello." She squeezed out a nervous smile as she looked up at him.

"Uh, it's good to see you again." He took off his hat slowly, and set it on the high-pommelled Western saddle in front of him. The wind caught at once at his black hair, combing it back off his high, smooth forehead. "How've you been?"

"Well, fine, I guess," she said, as awkward as he was. "Not bad."

"That's good. I'm glad to hear it."

"I rented a car in Trilby after we got off the train, but it broke down. I should have gone with one of the national companies. Mr. Thurrell offered to drive me from his garage, which was nice of him. He says he knew your father through some business dealings.''

She gestured back at the classic Caddy, knowing she was babbling. Alan was right to have insisted that she come out here and deal with the whole thing in person. She had ghosts to lay to rest—the ghosts of foolish dreams and fantasies, six months old, which Alan had understood better than she had. Alan Jennings was a sensible man, with a cool head on his shoulders.

That was why she planned to say yes, eventually, to his proposal of marriage. As soon as she'd dealt with just one small detail.

"Sorry you've had trouble," Gray said.

He must know why she was here. There was only one possible transaction that could take place between them. But it was time to put it into words. She took a deep breath.

"Gray, I'm sorry to bother you like this, when your letter said you were so busy, and all," she said apologetically, "but I really need that divorce."

"Mommy…" came Sam's plaintive little voice from the car at that moment.

Both adults turned their heads.

"That your little boy in there?" Gray asked. "Sam, isn't it?"

"Yes, that's Sam," Jill answered.

Gray gave a short nod, then added with a note of reluctance, "He sounds tired."

"Oh, exhausted!"

"It's a long trip for a kid."

"We're going to take a few days of vacation time on the way home." Alan was hoping to fly out and join them in Chicago for two nights, if he felt that his fledgling sales business could spare him.

"Okay." Gray nodded again.

Sensing his reluctance and interpreting it in the most obvious way, she said quickly, "I'm sorry just to show up like this."

"It's no problem, Jill. Really. It's my fault, far more than yours."

"You see," she went on, waving his objection aside, "I couldn't seem to track you down any other way. The phone number you gave me was disconnected. And anyway, I kind of thought I should come in person."

"We've rented out the main house now, and it took us a while to get the phone on down at the old place," he explained.

She sensed that there was more of a story to it than that, but kept her focus on the issue that concerned them both. "We need to discuss which state we're going to file in, for a start," she told him.

"Sure."

"I've researched the options—I spoke to a lawyer back in Philly—and I'm happy to do all the paperwork. If I head back into Blue Rock now with Mr. Thurrell and check in to a motel, is there any way you could come into town later today so we can talk? It shouldn't take long."

"Mommy..."

"I'm coming right now, sweetie." She turned back to the car, without waiting for a reply from the man who was—for the moment—her husband.

Behind her, Gray dismounted. Then he looped the

horse's reins around the top strand of wire, pressed the second strand down with one hand, scissored his leg back and climbed through. He'd been climbing through fences on this piece of land all his life, and it only took him a few seconds. Then he stopped and watched.

Jill had opened the rear door of the car and was leaning inside. This gave Gray a view of her neatly rounded behind that he didn't want to think too much about right now. He heard her speaking to her son in soothing, tender tones, and remembered how much he'd liked her voice in Las Vegas back in March.

There were a whole lot of things he'd liked about Jill Brown, when he stopped to think about it. One of the things he most definitely hadn't liked, however, was sitting right there in the Cadillac's rear seat. No ifs or buts, for a whole lot of reasons, he wasn't interested in a woman with a kid.

Even if he was married to her.

The way he was reacting to that appealing view of her behind, it would be a good thing if he kept this fact firmly in mind, he decided.

"I'm going to get you snuggled into bed as soon as I can, okay?" she said to her son. "We'll find you some kids' TV to watch, and some good food for you to eat."

"My head hurts."

"I know, sweetie. I have some Tylenol in our suitcase."

"Is he sick, or something?" Gray said, hearing the reluctance that thickened his voice.

Jill would probably think he was a callous son of a gun. He liked kids. He just didn't want one as part of a package deal, that was all. He hadn't known Jill had a son when he'd married her. Hell, he'd only found out her real name when they spoke their vows! The Las Vegas emcee had just kept calling her Cinderella.

Lord, thinking back, it had been a crazy setup, a crazy night, and the sooner they arranged their divorce, the better! She was right to have come out here, and he shouldn't have blown off her letter a few weeks ago, the way he had.

"H'llo, Gray." Ron Thurrell twisted in the car's front seat to acknowledge him with the muttered greeting, before returning to thumb through a mail-order catalog.

It seemed to be a signal to Gray and Jill that he was minding his own business, but Gray didn't trust it. He didn't like Ron, and the feeling was mutual. Ron was the man who had found Gray's father at the wheel of his car in Blue Rock's main street last December, in the grip of a severe stroke, and he'd been the one to call the ambulance for help. This had done nothing to strengthen their connection, however.

In fact, Gray was surprised that Ron had offered Jill a ride out here. Out of character, wasn't it? As for the "business dealings" with Dad, which Jill had hazily mentioned, as far as Gray knew they'd only ever consisted of Thurrell filling the gas tanks of various McCall vehicles.

Jill had turned at Gray's question, and he saw how tired and stressed she looked. Her dark, pretty hair was untidy, with little strands fluffing around her face. The jewel green of her eyes was intensified by the reddened rims. Her silky skin looked papery with fatigue, and she wore no makeup. Not that she needed it. She was just as pretty without it. But that generous bow of a mouth was too pale. A slash of color might have made her look happier.

She was ill at ease, too, which made sense if her son was sick and the only place she had to nurse him was Blue Rock's one motel. Gray had had to go sober up a seriously misbehaving ranch hand at that establishment once or twice, and he knew it was no place for a sick kid.

Jill didn't know it, though.

"I'm hoping it's just a twenty-four-hour virus," she said, in answer to what he'd asked. "As long as I can get him somewhere where it's quiet and warm...."

Nope. She definitely didn't know the Sagebrush Motel, nor the very rowdy bar attached to it.

"You can't go back into Blue Rock," Gray told her bluntly. "If I know C. J. Rundle, she won't even have the heat on yet."

"C.J....?"

"Proprietor of the Sagebrush Motel." He kept his voice low. "She's Ron's sister. And to call that place quiet is like calling Montana overpopulated."

"Isn't there somewhere else?" Her voice was pitched low, now, also.

"Only motel in Blue Rock," he answered. "You'd have to go on as far as Bozeman to get somewhere halfway decent."

"Okay," she began, nodding. "So if you could tell me the best place in Bozeman."

The movement of her nod was too vigorous and sharp, and her tone was too upbeat. He could tell she was fighting not to crumble, and he was horrified that she'd thought he was suggesting—

"Hey, I didn't mean that," he cut in quickly, his sympathy for her and the little boy surging. "You need to stay with us, is all. My mother and grandfather and me. We have plenty of space. It's nothing fancy, but your son...Sam...would have a bed with sheets that don't smell like forty years of cigarettes, and the furnace is lit, and my mom's probably cooking up a batch of beef and vegetable soup right this minute. Then you and I can settle the divorce thing tonight, while Sam's asleep, and you can get on your way once he's well enough to travel again."

He was making it all sound just a tad simpler than it was, and he hoped Sam would be well enough to travel again *soon*. The sooner he and Jill were out of each other's lives for good, the better for his peace of mind. Wincing inwardly, he wondered, *What the heck is Mom going to say when she discovers I'm married to this woman!*

"I—Lord, Gray, that would be so good!" Jill said, and her creamy voice shook. So did the fine-boned hand that came up to scrape some tickling strands of hair away from the corner of her mouth. "Do you really mean it?"

Gray wasn't going to waste time on one of those "Yes, I insist," "No, I couldn't trouble you" exchanges.

Instead, the only answer he gave was to open the front passenger door and say to Ron, "Thanks for doing this. Can you take her down to the old place? You know that's where we're living now?"

Most people in Blue Rock did know. Most of them probably had a good idea about why, also, although he and Mom and Grandpa were keeping as close-mouthed as they could about their dire financial state.

"I'd heard," Ron answered. "Of course." Then he shut his mouth abruptly, as if he'd have liked to say a lot more.

"I'll meet you there in a little bit, Jill," Gray said. "Just go ahead and introduce yourself to Mom and get yourself settled."

"If you're sure that—"

"No arguments."

"But I'm taking you away from your, uh, your ranch work, aren't I?" she answered, biting her lower lip. "Your cattle-branding, or whatever."

He didn't bother to tell her that they didn't generally brand cattle in Montana in September. He just said, with that same stiffness and reluctance still thickening his voice, "I was on my way back anyhow, to grab some lunch. I'm going to take a shortcut, down along the river. You'll get to the house first, but if you tell Mom I sent you, and that I'm coming along below the Angus spur, she'll make you welcome."

More welcome than I ever could.

"Weather's closing over," he finished, "and you need to get yourself and Sam inside."

"Okay, thanks Gray."

She looked like she was holding herself together with a Band-Aid, a cup of coffee and sheer force of will. "Did you hear that, Sammy?" she said to her son. "We're going to stay in a real ranch house tonight!"

The car door closed, and Ron wheeled the vehicle

back on to the rough track, snapping the dry gravel. Gray was left alone by the fence. He climbed back through, untied Highboy's reins, swung himself into the saddle and nudged the animal forward.

Recognizing that they were homeward bound at last, Highboy responded willingly, which left Gray free to think.

Damn it, he shouldn't be surprised that the crazy episode in Las Vegas had caught up with him at last! He'd known it would have to do so, sooner or later.

And it would have been sooner, if Jill's letter last month hadn't arrived the same day the McCalls' banker had told Gray once and for all that his loan was capped as it stood and there was no possible way to increase it any further, no more collateral he could use, no options left at all.

He had scribbled that quick note back to her on the counter at the post office. "I'm sorry, but I really don't have time to deal with it right now."

Generous of her to call it a letter. Then he had thought no more about it. His entire mind, in every waking moment, had been consumed with far more urgent concerns.

Their marriage was so bizarre, so unreal, so non-existent in any true sense. Did it really matter if they held off on the formality of a divorce for a little longer? Evidently it mattered to her, since she'd come all this way, and he felt bad about that, as he'd told her.

He should probably feel bad about their marriage, too. Angry at her for the way her stricken face had called to him that night and had made him act so impulsively. Angry at the cable TV station that had organized the "Cinderella Marriage Marathon" in a shameless attempt to climb onto the "reality TV" bandwagon.

But he didn't feel angry about that night. For some weird reason, their time together—all eight hours of it—was the only bright memory he had brought home from his ill-fated trip to Las Vegas in March.

Six months later, his body had awakened at once, clamoring with need at the very sight of her. Six months later, he could remember practically every word they'd spoken to each other, every gesture she'd made, every nuance of her laugh.

Six months later, however, and on his home ground, he was more realistic, more alive to his own vulnerability, and he just wanted beautiful, warm-hearted Jill Chaloner Brown out of his life.

Chapter Two

Jill thanked Mr. Thurrell for unloading her bag and went up to the house.

Thurrell cruised slowly off, without waiting until she'd reached the front steps. He seemed far more interested in watching a small group of cattle in a nearby field than in checking to see whether there was someone here to greet her. She felt very alone as she held feverish Sam awkwardly on her hip and hefted their shared travel bag in her other hand.

The setting of this house was magnificent. The Montana landscape awed her, dwarfing her concerns and mocking them at the same time. She'd never seen such incredible scenery. The mountains looked as though they had been painted onto the sky, huge and yet close enough to touch.

Overhead and in the distance to the east, clouds piled up and up into the blue. They were clouds like magic lands, tinted a hundred shades of white and gray. Their shadows chased across the straw-colored carpets of grass that covered the ground. To the west, higher up, they were different but just as beautiful, feathery and fast-moving against the high roofline of the house.

Beyond its gorgeous setting, the age and disrepair of the place showed, though. It hadn't been painted in so long that the clapboard was bare and weathered to a silvery gray. The wide front porch sagged.

Still, there was something appealing about the house. The porch was swept clean and set with a pretty harvest display of pale grasses, gourds in weird, goblin shapes and bunches of Indian corn. Surrounding the house like trusted companions were a half-dozen big old trees, and some wild and ancient rosebushes had recently had their long, supple canes trained and tied along the remains of a post and rail fence.

As Jill reached the porch, its swing creaked in the cold wind. The clouds that had been flying across the sky were beginning to change now. Grayson had been right about the weather closing over. Sam wasn't dressed for it, and his cheek was burning against hers. The need to get him inside, safe, warm, settled and filled with warm fluids overcame Jill's sudden attack of nerves, and she rapped on the door loudly, not really believing that anyone was home. The place was so quiet and solitary.

Until, blessedly soon, she heard footsteps. The door opened, and there stood an older female version of Gray, wearing jeans and an untucked shirt made of soft, plaid-patterned flannel. She had the same dark eyes and straight nose as her son, framed by a pretty cloud of gray hair.

Maybe she would have the same smile, too, only Jill hadn't seen that yet. Face to face with Mrs. McCall, she was overwhelmed by how much there was to explain, and by the need to cut it as short as possible in order to get Sam inside.

"Gray s-sent me," she stammered. "He's coming along the…I'm sorry…the Angus spur, I think he said. He'll be here soon. He said you'd— The thing is, my little boy is sick, and it's getting colder by the minute, and I really want to…"

She trailed off.

"It's all right. It's all right," said Mrs. McCall in a comfortable voice. Her hand, faintly dusted with flour, took Jill's travel bag and tucked it out of the way against the wall. The same hand left flour traces on Sam's forehead as she rested her palm there for a moment, then crooned, "You're as hot as can be, aren't you, cowboy? Come in, honey."

She put an arm around Jill's shoulder as Jill took a better hold on Sam, wrapping both her arms around him. He hadn't spoken a word since they left Gray back in that big open field.

"Come straight through to the kitchen," Gray's mother said. "I have the oven on, and it's the warmest room in the house. He must be hungry."

"I don't know if he is, but I'd like to get some hot liquid into him, and some Tylenol, and then I'm hoping he'll take a long nap. He hardly slept last night."

"Poor mite! I have soup on the stove and corn bread just gone into the oven. I've been expecting Gray back for lunch."

"We delayed him, I think."

"You'll eat, too?"

"As soon as I've settled Sam."

"You're staying the night, of course."

"Gray asked us to," Jill hedged, then admitted, "I was so grateful."

On her shoulder, Sam stirred. "Mommy...?"

"Isn't it good to be inside, Sam?" Jill whispered to him.

She dreaded the possibility that this was a real illness. Strep throat, or influenza. What were doctors like out here? How long would it be before he could travel safely?

Stomach in knots, she followed Gray's mother down a clean, plain hallway and, moments later, Sam was seated on her lap at a big old kitchen table. There was a cast-iron, wood-fired range that was no longer in use, next to an electric stove that wasn't a whole lot newer. There was a wooden dresser set with a motley collection of decorative plates, and there were floral calico curtains bunched in the windows.

Mrs. McCall moved about the large yet cozy room with quiet efficiency.

"Where did you leave Gray?" she said.

"Um, I'm not sure. About a mile back, I guess."

"He should be home any minute, then. He'll come and check that you're safe before he sees to the horse. You haven't told me your name yet, honey."

The reproof was so mild it was almost a compliment.

"I'm sorry. It's Jill. Jill Brown."

Jill Brown McCall? She didn't say it, being absolutely sure that Gray, like herself until very recently,

would have said nothing about their marriage to his
family.

"It's good to meet you, Jill. And you, Sam, darling-
heart, although I know you're feeling too bad to talk."
She slid a wide, half-filled soup plate across to Jill and
cautioned, "Still piping hot, so wait a little," then
added, "I'm Louise."

There was the sound of boots clumping on the back
steps, then the rattle and creak of old doors opening,
and Gray appeared. He swept his hat off his head with
a single, practised movement, and Jill could see that
his nose was shiny with cold and his black eyes glis-
tened. The feeling of the outdoor world of the ranch
seemed to enter the room with him. Space and air, the
smell of animals and grass, a sense of freedom coupled
with hard work.

The hard work part, Jill understood. She'd had to
work hard herself, for much of her life. She wasn't
afraid of work, and when she'd taken on a task, she
was stubborn about seeing it through. But everything
else about Grayson McCall was new. And appealing,
in an elemental way that unsettled and disturbed her.
Disturbed her far more than it had in Las Vegas, when
they'd both been playing roles that weren't their own.

She had to struggle to take her eyes off him, to ignore the way his muscles stretched beneath the fabric
of his clothing, and to avoid being aware of exactly
where he stood and how he moved in the room. Even
the sounds he made. The creak of his boots, the whoosh
of the breath he blew into his hands.

He shouldn't affect her in this way. Not when she
hardly knew him. Not when she sensed his reluctance

about having her here. And not the way things stood
in her life.

"That wind is *sharp!*" he said. "Mom, this is
Jill…and Sam."

"I know," Louise said easily. "We've just introduced ourselves."

"Can you make up some beds for them while I put
Highboy away?"

"You're not taking him out again later?"

"Going to look at the engine on the old pickup instead," he said, and Louise nodded but didn't say anything.

Jill realized that her arrival must have caused a
change in plans, casually communicated between son
and mother. But she understood too little about ranch
life to know if it mattered. She realized also that she'd
be even more of a nuisance if she protested.

*No, please, don't hold off birthing those ten dozen
calves, roping those six hundred steers and mending
that twenty mile fence on my account!*

Gray disappeared back out the kitchen door and his
mother went off to set up a bed for Sam. He would be
in it within minutes, Jill knew. Seated listlessly on her
lap, Sam was only eating the soup because she was
spooning it in. It smelled so good, and her own stomach was selfishly clamoring for its share.

Before the bowl was finished, Sam pushed the spoon
away and Jill didn't force the issue.

Louise McCall was back.

"All ready for him," she said. "I did yours, too, so
as not to disturb him later on. Now, what else do you
need before you get him settled?"

"Just a glass of water, please," Jill answered. "I want to give him some Tylenol, and he likes to wash away the taste afterward. Sam, sweetie, can you sit here while I find the Tylenol in our bag?"

He nodded, and sat obediently in the chair Jill had just vacated. From the far end of the hallway, as she rummaged around in their big canvas travel bag for the medicine, she heard Louise talking to him in a casual kind of way.

"I'm going to be here in the house all afternoon, little guy, so if you need anything you let me or your mom know, okay? And I should tell you, we have a cat might come and sleep on your bed, Sam. You like cats? Yeah, they're interesting creatures, aren't they? This one's old. She doesn't hunt anymore, just likes to find the warmest spot in the house and go to sleep. Will you mind if she does that on your bed?"

Bless her! Jill thought. *She must be wondering who in heaven we are and why we're here, but she hasn't asked a single question about it. Instead, all she wants to know is whether Sam feels safe with cats....*

And apparently Sam did, because the old tabby was already making herself comfortable on Sam's trundle bed as Jill got him undressed and snuggled into his stretchy pajamas, and Sam didn't object. Instead, as he slid between the covers, he croaked a tender "Hello, Firefly."

He curled his body to make room for the animal, whose purr was so loud it almost made the bed vibrate. Within seconds the two of them were lying there with eyes closed, heading for sleep.

Tear-blinded and shaky once more, Jill pulled the

faded, handmade quilt a little higher around Sam's shoulders and gave him a soft kiss. He was safe and cherished now in a way she hadn't dared to imagine an hour ago.

He'd probably be well again by the day after tomorrow, she decided. It was hope rather than science.

She went to the window, passing a neat pile of cardboard boxes, labeled with a black felt-tip pen. ''Dad's office,'' read several. ''Grandma's albums,'' said a couple more. A draught of warm air wafted up through the black metal grill of the heating vent in the floor, contrasting with the chilly vista through the window.

The clouds had lowered and thickened further, and had paled to a dull white which shrouded the tops of the mountains. Wind whipped the tethered canes of the roses and combed through the needles of the pines like distant singing.

Gray was coming across the yard. His hat was jammed down to cover his ears and his shoulders were hunched. His strides lengthened as he neared the house, as if he couldn't wait to get inside, and Jill had the strongest, strangest urge to hurry down to him, take his coat, serve him his soup and ask him about his day, as though she belonged here.

Considering that she was here to ask for a divorce, so she could be free to say yes to Alan, none of what she felt made any sense.

She made a stop at the bathroom on the way downstairs and noted that it resembled the rest of the house—old and shabby but scrupulously clean and brightened with homey touches that could only have been made by a loving hand.

When she reached the kitchen, Gray was at the table, chewing on warm corn bread and spooning in a huge bowl of soup.

"...couldn't have gotten it done this afternoon, anyhow, because it was a bigger problem than I'd thought," he was saying. "Wylie can't have checked it like he said he had." He hadn't heard or seen her arrival yet. "I'm going to have to bring you and Grandpa Pete with me, Mom, and I'm not sure how we're going to get the truck up there with the gear. 'S why I want to fix that oil leak and check the transmission, because otherwise we could get ourselves well and truly stuck."

Catching sight of Jill in the doorway, Louise McCall asked at once, "How is he, honey?"

Gray stopped eating and looked up at Jill. He gave a little nod of greeting, then watched her face with his dark eyes for a moment, before flicking his gaze downward. He hadn't waited for her reply to Louise's question. Didn't seem to want to know.

"He's asleep by now," she said. "Along with... with Firefly."

Ah, don't cry, Jill! she thought to herself angrily. *Why is this happening?*

"It's stupid," she went on, wiping tears onto her sleeve. "To cry about it, I mean. But I'm so grateful. Even your cat is making us welcome!"

"Well, why wouldn't we, Jill?" Louise said courteously. Then her curiosity got the better of her at last and she asked, "Are you in some kind of trouble, honey?"

"Mom, let's leave this till later, okay?" Gray growled, going back to his meal.

Both women ignored him. Jill fixed her gaze steadily on Gray's mother and said, "I was. At one time. And Gray helped me out. Which created a problem of its own, that I need help with. I promise I'll trouble you as little as I can. Sam getting sick was something I hadn't foreseen. It means we're going to be with you for a few days, when I'd been hoping I could start for home tomorrow."

"Don't worry about it," Louise said. "Please don't."

Her son didn't add the same assurance.

A silence fell, slightly awkward, as they finished their soup, which tasted every bit as good as it smelled. Gray wolfed down three bowls of it, along with substantial hunks of corn bread. He spoke just once more, to ask, "Grandpa's not coming back for lunch?"

"He took sandwiches and coffee," Louise answered. "Wants to get those cows moved down today."

"He shouldn't be doing it on his own."

Louise snorted. "You tell him that!"

Gray nodded and shrugged. "Guess I already did." As soon as he was done eating, he announced, "I'm going to get on over to the shed and look at that truck, or I won't get anywhere with it today."

"Can I help?" Jill blurted out. "Sam will sleep for hours now. He always does when he's feverish, so it doesn't make sense for me to sit around. You told him you'd be here at the house all afternoon, didn't you, Louise?"

Gray looked at her, as wary as before, and she could see the way he was assessing her words.

"Sure," he finally answered, much too slowly. "Can always use an extra pair of hands."

They set out ten minutes later. Jill was bundled up in an old scarlet sweater of Louise's. Louise had said that the shed was cold, and Jill's jacket and pink top "too pretty" to get covered in motor oil.

"You know anything about cars?" Gray asked her as they drove in his mom's late-model white station wagon back the same way Jill had come with Ron Thurrell.

"Not a whole lot," she admitted, "but I'm willing to learn."

"Not in one afternoon."

"No, okay, well, something else, then."

"You don't have to."

"You said you could use an extra pair of hands."

"I figured you wanted to come along so Mom didn't have a chance to ask you any more awkward questions."

"That was part of it," Jill admitted. "But I said I'd help, and I will."

The sound he made might have been, "Thanks."

Or it might have been a snort.

She lifted her chin and didn't push the point. Feeling the tension along her jaw, she glanced sideways and recognized much the same expression on Gray's face.

We're both stubborn, I guess, she thought.

Stubborn and honorable in his case. Stubborn and impulsive, in hers. Was that what had gotten them into trouble in Las Vegas?

Please get well quick, Sam. I'm here to dissolve the magic not make it stronger.

"Where are we headed?" she asked quickly.

"Machine shed," he answered. "We have a heavy-duty pickup we need to take cross-country to fix some fence. We've had cattle showing up where they don't belong."

"Like me."

"Really, Jill, you can quit apologizing." Impatience colored his tone. "I got us both into this as much as you did."

"Your mom would like to know what it's all about."

"Mom's pretty good, but she's only human."

"I know. It's not that I would have resented questions, I just didn't feel ready to answer them yet."

"Makes sense. Can I ask a couple?"

"Probably a little easier, coming from you," she agreed.

"You want to get married again, is that right? That's the only reason I could think of for the urgency."

"Uh, yeah." She listened to her own words, and realized that she had begun to adopt his own cautious, almost reluctant way of talking.

"I mean married for real."

"I know what you meant," she said. "Yes, married for real. I mean, we're not in love with each other, Alan and I. But when you have kids, that stuff's more trouble than it's worth. He knows that, and so do I."

"Yeah, I guess it could be that way," Grayson growled. "This guy has kids, too?"

"Teenage daughters, Anna and Sarah. And they come first. Them, and Sam. For both of us."

"Makes sense."

"Does it? I keep thinking you should be angry, Gray. Angry that this is happening at all. That I got you into it. In fact, on some level, you are angry."

"No, I'm not," he insisted. "Or, not with you. It's not your fault. Neither of us realized, when it was happening, that it was real...."

Real. Real as in legal. A very different kind of "real" from what she hoped to build with Alan.

The word echoed in Jill's mind, and she suddenly wondered if she had the slightest idea what "real" actually meant. She thought back...

Las Vegas. The show. "Cinderella on Ice." A dream come true. A dream made real. Only, from the very beginning, it hadn't been.

Jill had skated since she could remember, pushed into it at first by her selfish and demanding mother, then loving it for its own sake. She had found a home away from home at the rink, when life with her mother, Rose Chaloner Brown, had been like a minefield that all beloved stepfather David Brown's care and sense couldn't make safe, and all of her sisters' companionship couldn't distract from.

Rose had kicked her out the door when she was pregnant and alone at just eighteen, along with her stepsister, Catrina, who was almost Jill's twin in age. Jill's older sister, Suzanne, had refused to stay under a roof where her sisters weren't welcome, so she'd left at that time, also.

"Ungrateful," Rose had called all three of them. She'd used much harsher labels, as well.

After this, the expense of Jill's competitive amateur career had been way too much for the sisters' stretched finances. So she had concentrated on teaching as a fall-back, while dreaming of the chance to skate in professional shows.

She had had Sam to raise, also. He was still the best thing that had ever happened to her, despite the disaster of her naive infatuation for his father. None of it had been easy, though. Ivy League boyfriend Curtis Harrington hadn't wanted to know about the coming baby. Jill didn't know how she would have managed if she hadn't had Suzanne's and Catrina's help, as well as that of Catrina's eccentric Cousin Pixie, for the past couple of years.

Back in March, just after Sam's fourth birthday, she'd gotten her big break at last. Andrea, a close friend during their teens at the ice rink in Philadelphia, had been forced to pull out of her role in "Cinderella on Ice" for six weeks, due to an injury. The one-sided contract Andrea had signed stipulated that she'd lose her place in the show permanently unless she could come up with a temporary replacement of her own.

Enter Jill Brown, with stars in her eyes.

She had left Sam in the loving care of her sisters and flown out to Las Vegas to step onto the ice as a Featured Mouse and Cinderella understudy. And she had hated every minute of it. Her dreams were shattered. She felt like a fool for thinking that a showgirl lifestyle, so incompatible with Sam's needs, could have made her happy.

The show was a cheap takeoff of the far more glamorous Disney version. The performers were badly paid and badly treated, and tensions between the cast members were high. Jill had missed Sam more than she'd have thought possible, every minute of every day. The knowledge that he was happy and well cared for with Cat, Suzanne and Pixie didn't help.

She was supposed to endure almost six more weeks of this?

Maybe it should have helped when Trixie, the regular Cinderella, came down with a bad dose of flu on Jill's first Saturday in Las Vegas. To skate as Cinderella should have been a dream come true, but it wasn't.

Lying in bed in a darkened room, Trixie had overwhelmed Jill with advice and instructions, in a pained, croaky voice. "And don't forget that publicity thing afterward. The 'Cinderella Marathon' thing."

"What?"

"The ball thing, the contest, with the cable channel."

"I don't know anything about that."

"You just have to stick around the hotel. It's in the big function room. You're the so-called 'Celebrity bride.' They'll tell you what to do. You haven't heard about it? There's been a lot of publicity about the rules and prizes, and all."

"No, I haven't heard about it." *I've been too busy crying into my pillow, missing Sam and wishing I'd never come.*

"It's no big deal, but you know management will kill you if you don't show."

"I know."

So she had "shown" for the "Cinderella contest thing" in the big function room just as she was supposed to do, without the slightest idea what it was all about....

"This is it," Gray said, wheeling the pickup to a halt in front of a big metal shed.

Jill was impressed by the sizeable collection of buildings grouped nearby. She could only guess what they were used for. Milking? Did the McCalls run the kind of cattle that got milked? Somehow, she thought not.

In the distance, she could glimpse the large new house on the hill, the place that the McCalls were renting out in order to stretch their cash flow a little. It was separated from this section of the ranch by three fences and a line of healthy young trees, their leaves ablaze with fall color.

Gray jumped out of the truck, and she watched him for a moment before getting out herself. He was such a capable looking man, as upright and sturdy as a tree trunk, both in body and heart, but she had known from the moment they met that he was hurting. Something in his life wasn't right, and he had his back to the wall as he fought his circumstances.

She didn't know the whole story, but she knew some of it, thanks to the way they'd talked that night in Las Vegas six months ago. His father had overstretched their finances with the purchase of a neighboring ranch immediately before his death. As a result, Grayson, his newly widowed mother and his fit but elderly grandfather were in danger of losing the land that had been in the McCall family for over eighty years.

Until seeing the place for herself today, Jill hadn't been able to grasp what that meant. Now, she was just beginning to understand. This place was substantial, beautiful, and expensive to run—rewarding of success and dramatically unforgiving of failure.

And somehow the thought of Gray failing, of losing the fight to save his family ranch after the blow of his father's death, suddenly mattered to her. It mattered in a way that made her throat tighten and took her breath away. She didn't want to think of him failing after such a struggle, through no fault of his own.

This was what the word "real" meant, she understood.

"Real" wasn't the bewildering whirl of their publicity-stunt Cinderella marriage, under the glare of TV lights. The marriage was legal, as Jill's lawyer had advised, but it wasn't real. "Real" wasn't even the unexpected moment of stillness in the midst of it all. The moment when she and Gray had said their vows, still believing them to be a meaningless charade, and had looked into each other's eyes and felt...*magic.*

None of those things were real. But this... *This* was real. Gray's struggle to keep his ranch and the life he loved was real. No wonder he just wanted to sign those divorce papers, watch Sam get quickly well and wave them goodbye.

Alan was right, she thought. *He knew I couldn't get the magic of that night with Gray out of my head. He knew I had to come here and feel the reality for myself.*

Chapter Three

"You don't have to work so hard, Jill," Gray said.

He had been glancing up from beneath the hood of the pickup to watch her every few minutes for the past hour and a half. He hadn't seen her take a break yet.

When they reached the shed, she had insisted on a "real job." Hiding his skepticism, he'd taken her at her word. It hadn't been hard to find one for her. She was chipping off rust-blistered paint and coating a de-rusting treatment onto the bale retriever. The vehicle was falling apart but it had to last out a whole season of winter feeding. There was no way he could afford to get it replaced as his father had planned to do this year.

Some of those rust patches were getting downright dangerous. They had begun to eat into and weaken the metal, and she was taking it seriously. He was amazed at how hard she was prepared to work. She had chips of yellow paint all over Louise's old red sweater, and a streak of rust across her cheek. The air smelled of the acrid chemical treatment. The noise she had made as she chipped was like fingernails on a chalkboard.

Jill's neat hips moved in rhythm as she worked. Her pert derriere stuck out when she bent to reach an awkward spot with her brush. Louise's sweater hugged her figure soft and close, showing her curves. The sight once again affected Gray in a way that was both delicious and uncomfortable.

From time to time she shook her glossy dark hair back out of her eyes. Once she wiped her hands on a rag and re-wound the piece of pink elastic around her jaunty ponytail to keep it more securely out of the way. The movement lifted the neat swell of her breasts, and lifted the sweater to briefly show an inch of silky skin around her waist.

Gray knew women—ranchers' wives and daughters included—who would have thrown up their hands at the job long ago, but Jill was taking it all in stride. Or maybe she was just releasing pent-up tension. This situation couldn't be any easier for her than it was for him. She was stuck here on the ranch with a sick child, when all she wanted was to make an arrangement about the divorce and get on with her life.

He closed the hood of the pickup and went over to her.

Short of investing in parts he couldn't afford—like a whole new engine, maybe—he'd done all he could to make the truck worthy of a grinding ride into one of the roughest sections of the entire ranch. He had gone out on horseback this morning, hoping for a quick fix with a few coils of wire. Instead he was going to need new posts, new holes and half a dozen heavy tools.

It was just one more task he didn't need, with all his ranch hands laid off and his grandfather working way harder than an old man should. Not to mention Mom.

"I'm doing fine here," Jill told him.

She straightened. He could see a tiny yellow paint chip on her jaw line that his fingers itched to brush away. He remembered all too clearly how soft her skin was in that spot.

"I know you are," he answered instead. "You've done a great job. I never thought you'd get that far in a couple of hours. But we should pack up now and head back. It's getting dark out."

She blinked. "That late?"

"Time flies when you're having fun."

"Ha ha."

"While we're clearing up, shall we grab a coffee and talk a little bit?"

"Sure. About the divorce?"

"And about the marriage. Square our stories. How much do you want to tell Mom?"

He went over to a bench at the side of the shed, where there was a sink and a faucet and a propane camping stove.

"It's your decision, Gray," she answered.

"I'm inclined to keep it simple." He added water to a kettle and instant coffee granules to two cups as he spoke. "Let's just say you got in trouble with a contract in Las Vegas that I was a witness to, and now there are some legal papers for me to sign so you can get out of the situation. That's...kind of the truth."

She laughed. "Sort of kind of, I guess."

"Okay, I admit it." He spread his work-roughened hands and gave an upside down smile. "I'm embarrassed to tell my mother that I actually *married* a woman I hadn't even met purely because I felt sorry for her!"

"You didn't know it would be legal."

"Might have done it anyway, under the circumstances," he growled.

She raised her eyebrows. Didn't quite believe him.

"Well, I'm grateful," she said. "I'll never forget how it felt to escape from those other guys, Gray, when I realized they weren't prepared to go over five hundred dollars and you were."

"How'd you know I wasn't a creep, too?"

It was something he had been wondering on and off for six months. How they had *both* known, actually, that it was a good deed on his part. That he was saving Cinderella, not kidnapping her.

She went still at his question, and her jewel green eyes rounded. "I—" She stopped, and laughed her pretty, golden laugh. "Lord, you know, I never even thought about that. I...just knew."

She looked at him and frowned. Her head tilted slightly to one side as if she was tallying his attributes. He met her gaze steadily, but felt self-conscious. He wasn't sure what she would think about what she saw.

He was a simple man, big, strong, but with no airs and graces. He wore work clothes six and a half days a week, and he had rough hands like two fresh offcuts of wood. There was no glamour attached to him. He couldn't be the type she was used to—like the man in Pennsylvania who wanted to marry her, for example.

"I guess because you were just sitting there quietly," she said finally.

"Yeah, I'd just come in for a beer," he agreed, remembering...

He had made the journey to Las Vegas in desperation. He wanted to see his older half-brother, Mitch, who was the only person he could think of who might lend him the money he needed to put capital into the expanded. Thurrell Creek, owned by Wylie Stannard for thirty years since he'd won it from Ron Thurrell's father in a bet, was run down and neglected and in very bad shape.

If he could put some money into Thurrell Creek, if the weather was kind to him, if he didn't lose too many calves, then he'd have cattle to sell and could hopefully claw himself up out of the hole the ranch was buried in.

Why had Dad suddenly bought Thurrell Creek from old Wylie Stannard last December, when Wylie had blown into town from back east, ready to sell? Had Dad stopped to think about quite how much it would stretch their cash flow? Did he have a strategy for making it work?

Nine months later, Gray still didn't know.

By a chilling coincidence, which still sent prickles up his spine whenever he thought of it, Frank McCall had died that same day. He and Stannard and the McCalls' lawyer, Haydon Garrett, had finalized the purchase of the ranch. Afterward, on his way home, Frank had suffered what would prove to be a fatal stroke, at the wheel of his pickup in Blue Rock's main street. He'd never been able to talk about the purchase of Thurrell Creek, and how he planned to manage.

But if Dad thought we could do it, then we should be able to do it. Gray had thought this way in Las Vegas, and he was still thinking this way now. *Is it my fault? Was he that much better a rancher than I am? We had a tough winter. We lost more stock than I'd hoped. We had to replace the generator, and we had that fire in the feed store. But Dad was the one who taught me to allow for contingencies like that.* Why *did he think we could stretch ourselves so thin?*

Gray had not told Mitch any of this when he made his desperate plea for funds. It didn't change the outcome. Mitch refused to help.

Sitting defensively behind his desk in his big office in downtown Vegas, Mitch had told his half-brother angrily, "Your father told me to stay out of your lives."

"Yes, because—"

"Now, suddenly, when Frank is gone—" Mitch plowed through Gray's words "—and you need my money, the money I made in business with my own father, it's a different story."

"It's not like that, Mitch. Dad spoke in anger that day." Gray didn't add his opinion that Frank McCall's anger had been more than justified after the years of hurt Mitch had inflicted on the family, both before and after his departure from the ranch at the age of nineteen. "You know they both wanted to heal the rift. Mom hoped so much that you'd come to Dad's funeral. She phoned you. She begged—"

"It was too late for that," Mitch cut in, his mouth tight. "Mom's always been too sentimental. She may believe that anger shouldn't last beyond the grave, but that's not my opinion."

What could Gray do at this point but accept defeat? He didn't know which was worse—that he hadn't found a way to save the ranch, or that Mitch and Louise were still so deeply at odds, with himself, as Frank's son, locked in the middle. Both facts had his gut tied in knots, and he hadn't trusted himself to drive after he left Mitch's office. Had decided to stay overnight, start heading back at first light.

By that time, it was late afternoon, and he'd wandered into the gaming and entertainment section of his hotel, emotions stretched tight as a fiddle string. He'd fed five dollars into a slot machine, purely for the release of hearing the strident noise as he pulled the handle. He had received six hundred dollars worth of winnings from his last pull with an absent sort of surprise. At least it covered the cost of the trip.

But the slot machines and blackjack tables held no real appeal, and he didn't go back for more. Instead, he ended up nursing two free beers and watching "Cinderella on Ice," purely to eat up some more time, take his mind off his troubles.

And that was where he'd first seen Jill Brown, skating her heart out in the title role. Her body was trim and athletic and feminine in a glittering costume. Her smile was so dazzling and electric it could have powered up the expensive new generator in back of the machine shed six times over. Every gesture she made was graceful and heartfelt. She was incredible.

The memory had stayed inside him, warm and bright, when he left the show. And he'd carried it with him as he'd ended up in the adjacent ballroom, in search of a final beer.

"I was passing the time," he said to Jill, still remembering. "Feeling wound up and knowing I wouldn't sleep yet. Didn't know they were going to be launching into that stunt."

"And you weren't drunk, and you didn't have your greedy eyes on the prizes, like most people did."

True, the prizes were impressive. A luxury car, a palatial home and a two-week cruise for the couple that stayed married the longest. Each couple had to sign a statement that they were strangers to each other before the ceremony, a fact which would be checked out later on. The development of their relationship would then be filmed and shown daily on TV. Last couple left standing would win.

Back home in Montana, Gray had tuned in to the "Cinderella Marriage Marathon" several times over the past six months, and had kept tabs on the progress of the competition. Of the ten couples who'd started out, only two were still left, and in both relationships the cracks were widening and the strain was showing. One couple was practically at each other's throats, but they wouldn't give up. America was fascinated.

Jill and Gray hadn't taken note of the competition rules before the ceremony and hadn't wanted to take part in it afterward. Each of them had felt, without needing to put it into words, that the price to be paid for those prizes was far too high. They'd signed their intention to seek a divorce almost immediately. The camera team assigned to them had stopped filming them seconds later.

"And I wasn't playing up to the whole thing like all the other girls were," Jill went on, "because they were so desperate to get chosen. I figured you wouldn't be bidding for me if you thought a good time was part of the package, because it had to be pretty obvious I wasn't planning on giving you one."

"You gave me a great time that night, Jill," Gray said quietly.

"I—Well, yes, me too." She flushed a little, beneath the streaks of rust and flecks of paint. "But you know what I mean."

He nodded. He knew exactly what she meant.

He could still picture the whole scene. To follow the Cinderella theme, they'd set it up as a ball, with a token ten minutes of dancing so that the entrants could "get to know each other." Then the organizers had quickly gotten down to business. There were about a dozen guys bidding, though a couple of them dropped out without making a match. And there were about twice that many girls, complete with their own wedding dresses.

Jill was billed as the "Celebrity Cinderella" and a minor actor and body-builder flown in from Los Angeles was the "Celebrity Prince." Gray had had no intention whatsoever of taking part. In fact he'd been on the point of gulping his last mouthful of beer and hightailing it out of there.

But then he'd seen the way Cinderella looked. In contrast to all the others, she didn't want to be there. Didn't want to be part of it. She had skated with such an appealing blend of soul, grace and pizzazz, earlier. But at the ball, she looked miserable and frozen. The cheesy type who was emceeing the event and egging the participants on had had to lean on her pretty hard at one point to get her to put on a better face.

Which she had. She had the most beautiful wide, white, sparkly smile, when she could manage to sustain it.

But Gray wasn't fooled. He was close enough to the action that he could still see her green eyes. Bidding for Cinderella had quickly narrowed down to himself and a couple of loud, crude guys who seemed too drunk to even realize that she wasn't promising to put out that night, the way the other girls were. Gray had won her, finally, for five hundred and twenty dollars. He had then gone up to the stage to endure what he had presumed to be a mock ceremony.

They had both signed some papers and made some vows. Strange, those vows. For one weird, suspended moment, he'd almost felt like he meant them. Had to be because of the atmosphere of lights and music and glamour and excitement, he decided.

Maybe stress and fatigue, too. His mind was playing tricks on him. It hadn't been an easy day. It was only afterward, when the camera crew honed in on them, that he and Jill had asked a few crucial questions and realized what they'd gotten themselves into.

"You want to sign off?" one of the organizers had asked.

"We want to sign off," they'd both agreed at once.

After the camera had moved away, the organizer had added, "Yeah, we never expected the celebrity couples to try to win. We put you in for the publicity, Cinderella, but there's been such a buzz with this thing we could have done it without that.''

He'd written each of them a modest check ''for expenses.'' Like the cost of the divorce?

''It'll be a formality, wherever you file,'' he had told them. ''And you're lucky. The regular couples don't get expenses when they drop out.''

''Dropped *out?*'' one of the other new brides had shrieked, overhearing the last two words. ''You've dropped out already? Are you insane? This is the chance of a lifetime! Have you seen the pictures of that house? It really is a palace!''

''I—I— No, I—'' Jill had frozen, and the other bride's camera crew was practically in her face.

Gray had shoved the check in his jeans pocket, grabbed her hand and pulled her off the stage, out of the crowded ballroom and out of the hotel as fast as he could. They'd walked for a good ten minutes in silence past the oddly beautiful neon signs and splashing fountains of the hotels before she'd finally said a single, simple ''Thank you.''

Then they'd found a quiet corner in a noisy diner and talked over coffee until dawn.

''Anyway,'' Jill said now, breaking a silence. ''The divorce. It isn't quite as easy as that guy made out. I spoke to a lawyer about the various options. I told you that, didn't I?'' She sipped her coffee, but didn't look as if she was tasting it. ''An annulment's no good. In most states, for a civil marriage, that's only applicable in cases of fraud. And Nevada doesn't work for a divorce. One of us would need to be a resident there for six weeks, which I can't afford to do and I'm sure you can't either, can you?''

Her hopeful intonation made it clear she somehow thought he might. But he had to kill that idea immediately.

"Six weeks?" He laughed briefly. "Couldn't afford six hours away from this place, right now!''

"No, I didn't think so." Her face fell. "If we do it through the Montana legal system, apparently, there has to be serious marital discord with no prospect of a reconciliation, or we have to be separated and apart for more than one hundred eighty consecutive days.''

"So have we just blown that by your coming here and staying in my house until your kid gets better?''

She was completely silent for about five seconds, then swore mildly but very effectively.

"That still leaves us with serious marital discord,'' Gray pointed out helpfully.

"Trouble is, there isn't any. I—I really don't feel that bad about you, Gray,'' she told him almost timidly. "I mean, you know, this whole thing just *happened....*''

"And you want to *un*-happen it with as little fuss as possible?''

"Exactly. I don't want to have to pretend that we're at each other's throats. So I guess that leaves Pennsylvania, where I was told that a mutual consent, no-fault divorce takes four to five months.''

"I like the sound of that.''

"Except the four to five month part. Alan wants to— We *both*,'' she corrected quickly, "want to get on with our lives.''

"Think you're just going to have to bite the bullet on this one, Jill," Gray said slowly. "There's nothing else we can do about it."

"You're right." She didn't look happy. "Well, I brought the Pennsylvania papers with me in case that's what we decided on, so you can sign them when you have a spare moment, and then we can handle the rest by mail."

They left the machine shed five minutes later, in an atmosphere of awkwardness and vague sadness that Gray couldn't quite put his finger on, and didn't like one bit.

Still asleep.

Jill stood by Sam's bed for a minute or two, chewing on her lip. He was still flushed and feverish. She wondered how far the nearest doctor was. Not that she was deeply concerned yet. He often started a head and chest cold with a day of fever. If he'd developed a runny nose by tomorrow and his fever had gone, it would be a familiar pattern.

Louise had reported that Sam hadn't stirred during the afternoon. Firefly was gone from the bed, however. Jill was afraid Sam would be frightened when he awakened in the unfamiliar room, so she left a trail of lights on, from the low lamp on the dresser to the wall lights on each level in the stairs and hallway, and through into the kitchen.

Louise was cooking up a storm. She had made a vast stew, soup, spaghetti sauce, chicken casserole and several pies. There were steaks spitting on the griddle and a bowl of baked potatoes steaming on the table.

She was ladling the stew into several plastic food
storage containers and talking ranch business with an
elderly man who sat at the table. This must be Gray's
grandfather. He looked tired, and there were red
patches of windburn on his cheeks. They both stopped
talking when they saw Jill.

"Can I help?" she offered automatically.

"I'm just about done," Louise answered. "I'm
cooking up a whole batch of meals so we can still eat
well when I go out with the men to work the ranch.
Gray told us you put in a pretty good stint yourself
today. He says you didn't stop the whole afternoon."

"Too cold in that shed to sit still," Jill joked.

"Did you want to wash up before dinner?"

"Gray's in the bathroom right now. I got in before
him and cleaned the bits that show."

Louise laughed. "This is my dad, Jill," she said.
"Gray's grandfather, Pete Marr."

"It's good to meet you, Mr. Marr," Jill said, and
took the sinewy hand he held out to her.

He simply nodded, then turned to Louise again.
"Best wash up, myself. I can hear Gray up in his room,
now. Down again in a minute."

He loped rather stiffly from the room, and the silence
in his wake was a little awkward, till Louise said, "You
mustn't mind if he doesn't say much. He gets so tired
and, well, I don't think he's ever going to get used to
the changes that have come since Frank's death. They
were fond of each other, those two."

She looked up from the container she was filling and
Jill saw the dry, helpless anguish in her eyes, beyond
the capable, maternal facade. She had to fight an im-

pulse to go and hug the older woman, as if she belonged here and the problems that had come since Frank McCall's death were problems she shared.

It was a relief when Gray entered. He had changed into fresh jeans, fastened with a big silver belt buckle, and a blue plaid western shirt that fitted tight across his broad shoulders. His black hair was still damp from his shower and rumpled from the towel.

Something twisted like a snake inside Jill. It was a coil of physical need that she hadn't felt in a long time. She didn't want to feel it now. Not for Grayson McCall.

He looked straight toward her, as if he could tell what she was feeling, and her skin began to prickle with awareness. She wanted to shout at him, "Don't! Stop reading me, and understanding me. I'm not a part of your life, and I never will be. Don't waste your precious energy. You need it for more important things."

Instead, as if he'd asked about her son, she said quickly, "Sam's still asleep. Your mom says he's hardly stirred. I hope that means he's sleeping off his fever."

"Do you think he'll need to see a doctor?"

"If he's still feverish tomorrow."

"Okay." He nodded, his face closed.

"Is there one close?"

"Blue Rock," Gray said.

"I guess around here that's close," she agreed.

The steaks were done, and Louise had finished batching up her pre-cooked meals. She slung a big bowl of salad onto the table, as well as sour cream for

the potatoes and a bottle of blue cheese salad dressing.
Gray began laying plates and glasses and silverware.
His grandfather appeared again and they all sat down.

Conversation came in fits and starts, but it didn't feel
awkward. The food was too good, the kitchen too
warm, and the sense of caring between Gray, his
mother and grandfather too strong and real for awkwardness.

Afterward, Jill helped Louise to clear up. Then she
took a hot shower and went early to bed, knowing
she'd be up in the night with Sam. Sure enough, he
awoke at ten, hungry enough for some soup with fingers of toast. He was hot enough to need more Tylenol
as well. He was asleep again by eleven. Jill slept, too,
soon afterward.

Jill had spent years rising before dawn to train at the
ice rink, and she wasn't surprised when she awoke at
the first hint of daybreak.

Ranchers rose early, too, she soon discovered. Gray
was already in the kitchen. He had coffee brewing in
a coffee maker, scrambled eggs cooking and bacon siz-
zling on the stove. Above the sharp spitting noise, he
didn't hear Jill enter. At the sound of her tentative,
creaky-voiced greeting, he whirled around, astonished.
He held his hands away from his sides like a gunslinger
about to draw.

"I'm sorry," he said roughly. "I didn't mean to
waken you."

"You didn't," she told him. "I'm used to waking
early. Don't look so surprised!"

"Guess I kind of assumed you had to be a night owl."

"Because of the situation in Vegas?" she guessed, then went on quickly, "That wasn't my life, Gray. Don't ever make the mistake of thinking that was my life."

"I know. I guess I did know that," he conceded. "I shouldn't have been surprised. Want to squeeze some orange juice?"

"Sure."

She didn't resent his quick change of subject. He was busy. Obviously he had to get outside to work as soon as he could. But he needed a man's breakfast first. She got several oranges from a bowl on the big table and picked up the knife he'd slid across to her. She began to slice the oranges in half. A fresh, sweet citrus smell added to the salty tang of the bacon.

There was a short silence, then he said, "We talked all night in that diner. About this time of the morning, you were getting ready to go to bed."

"And you were going to head off in your truck."

"That's when I got sleepy. Had to stop for a couple of hours and take a nap, with the steering wheel for a pillow."

"And I had to get up five hours later to be ready for a two o'clock show."

"So we were both crazy that night," he agreed. "Staying awake like we did."

He bent down, got a plastic jug with a juicing top out of a drawer and passed it to her. She reached for it too soon and grabbed his warm, callused fingers as well. They both apologized, then laughed, and it was

awkward. Jill heard creaking upstairs, and wished that
Louise or Grandpa Pete would come down quickly and
chaperone them.

The kiss.

That was the problem. That was the reason for this
sudden awkwardness. Both of them were thinking
about the kiss.

Staying up all night to pour out your heart to the
stranger whom you'd just married was crazy enough,
but sealing it all with a kiss was crazier still. That part
should never have happened.

Out the kitchen window, it was fully light although
the first rays of the sun had not yet beamed above the
surrounding mountains. It was just this time of day
when they had left the diner. Gray wanted to get back
to his hotel to check out. The run-down motel room
Jill shared with two of the other skaters was in the
opposite direction, so this was the moment of parting.

It was chilly. The desert air cooled dramatically at
night. Dew fell from a clear sky. Las Vegas dawns in
March were gorgeous—bright and fresh and cold. Jill
was still wearing last night's designer wedding gown.
It was a dramatically draped piece of cream silk, lent
by a local bridal store in return for some free advertis-
ing, and it was gorgeous. Not exactly warm, but Gray
had lent her his jacket hours earlier when they left the
bride auction, so she wasn't cold.

It must have looked strange, though, that rich silk
gleaming below the rough, dark jacket that reached
down to her thighs. A cowboy bride, ready to rope
cattle in a wedding gown.

She remembered how reluctant she had been to take

the jacket off. Not just because she didn't want the cold to strike her bare skin. Not because she didn't want to have to walk back to her nearby motel with a bared neck. It was more than that.

She'd found a special sense of safety wrapped inside the garment. The shoulders were way too wide. The sleeves were way too long. But the warmth of it was more than physical. It was like being wrapped in Grayson McCall's big, capable arms.

And now it was time to surrender all this, the last remnant of the magic. Slowly, she had begun to pull apart the snaps, and had shivered in anticipation.

"Keep it for now," he'd said suddenly. "Mail it back to me. I gave you my address."

"No, Gray, I—"

"Keep it," he'd insisted.

So she had nodded silently, looking up into his face, and she'd known he was going to kiss her a good thirty seconds before it actually happened....

"Shoot!" Gray said. He hadn't been concentrating and he'd splashed what had to be a half-cup of bacon fat onto the back of his hand.

Idiot! he chided himself. He went at once for the faucet and plunged his stinging hand under the flowing water to cool the burn and minimize the damage. That would be just great, wouldn't it? If he didn't look after this properly, it could get infected, put him and his hand out of action for a couple of days. Even with his quick reaction, it was going to hurt today when he worked.

He knew why he hadn't been concentrating. He was

thinking about that kiss. So was she. The air was thick and warm with memory. It was helped along by the dramatic, atmospheric Montana dawn breaking outside the kitchen window.

Hell, he remembered every second of it in every detail, although it was six months ago, now. The way her nose had been cold as it bumped against his cheek. The way her mouth had been so plummy and sweet and warm, just as he'd known it would be. The way her fingers had lifted to thread through his hair, the little noise she'd made in her throat and the swish of the rich fabric as they moved together. The way his jacket had dwarfed her slim body. She'd mailed it back as promised, and it had arrived at the ranch just two days after he did.

"Let me see that burn, Gray," Jill demanded, concern filling her voice. "It looks nasty."

"Cold water's the best thing."

"I know, but not just running it under the faucet like that. Let me fill a bowl. Is it blistering?"

"Don't think so. I reacted pretty fast."

"You did, but that bacon fat has congealed on your skin. Let me wash it off, or it'll seal in the burn."

She filled the bowl he'd mixed the eggs in. He put his hand into it and stood helplessly as she grabbed a spurt of detergent and lathered it across the backs of his fingers and down toward his wrist. The white grease mapped the area of the burn. It brought home to him that her concern was well-founded. The burn was bigger than he'd thought, and all because he'd been thinking about their kiss.

He still was.

Their hands had touched, just as they were doing now. They had laced their fingers together, and their joined hands had gotten ambushed by the folds of her dress as he'd leaned closer. He'd stepped six inches forward to bring his legs hard against hers. He'd wanted to capture her, capture the moment and the memory forever.

They must have looked a sight, standing outside that diner. The cowboy and his Las Vegas Cinderella bride, kissing in the light of the sun's first rays, her in his jacket and him practically wearing her dress, because its skirt was so full and he was standing so close.

Ah, but he hadn't cared what they looked like. He hadn't cared about anything. For that one long, stretched out minute, nothing else had existed in the world but her sweet body and her sweet lips and her sweet voice saying his name.

"Gray? Gray, I think the eggs are burning."

"Yeah, they would be," he muttered.

He took his clean and grease-free but still throbbing hand out of the water and lunged back to the stove. Jill rescued the bacon before it suffered the same fate as the eggs. A few minutes later, they had toast in the toaster, and coffee poured out, and scrambled eggs piled on plates with the worst of the burned part still stuck to the pan. Things were starting to appear completely under control once more.

But somehow this only made the timing seem more perfect when Louise's footsteps stopped creaking the floorboards upstairs and approached along the hallway instead.

"Jill?" she began as soon as she reached the kitchen doorway.

"Yes, Louise?"

"Sam was stirring, so I went in and checked on him and it was obvious when I took one look at his face what the problem was yesterday."

"It was?"

"Honey, he has the chicken pox!"

Chapter Four

Jill and Gray took Sam to the doctor in Blue Rock mid-morning, for an eleven-o'clock appointment.

By this time, his chicken pox were growing in number so fast Jill thought she'd be able to see them popping up like air bubbles in a half-cooked pancake if she stopped still long enough to look. He was still feeling very sorry for himself. Worse than he had felt yesterday, she decided unhappily.

His fever was up over 102 until she gave him some more Tylenol to bring it down, and he complained of a headache. He had no appetite or energy, and he had to be persuaded into the bath. Jill was a little skeptical herself about the bath at first. Louise had cut the leg off an old pair of her pantyhose and filled it with a generous handful of oatmeal.

"Squeeze it in the water," she told Jill, who was kneeling by the old-fashioned white claw-foot tub.

"You'll see the starch coming out. It looks like milk and it'll soften the water and ease the itching."

It felt like making mud pies. The starch was gooey and creamy as Jill squeezed it through her fingers. Sam summoned enough energy to want to do it himself. "Can't I, Mom? It looks like fun."

So she handed the ball of nylon-covered oatmeal to him. She looked up at Louise after a minute or two, when the water was milky white. "I never knew about this. Does it really work?"

"Like a charm," Louise said, standing in the bathroom doorway. "Both my boys had chicken pox at around this age, and they don't have a single scar."

"I guess my mom didn't know about it, then, because I've got quite a few," Jill said.

"Only in places where they don't show," Gray said, appearing behind his mother. Then his face filled with horror as all three of them heard the suggestive implication in the words. "I mean, not that I've— There's none on your face, is what I mean. Your skin is—I'm done, is what I wanted to say, Jill, and ready to head into town."

"Sure. Um…" She was even more flustered than he was. She nodded energetically, stood up, turned around, came to a halt. "Sam is—"

"No hurry. I'll grab some coffee and a bite to eat. We've got another half hour or so before we really have to leave."

"Okay."

"I'm taking your car, Mom. Are you coming, too?"

"No, but I have quite a list of things you can pick up for me."

Jill relaxed a little at these words from Louise. At least it didn't seem as if the trip into town was purely for Sam's sake.

It was ten o'clock, now, more than four hours since Gray's huge dawn breakfast, and he had been working out of doors for all of that time. Jill didn't know what he'd been doing. She had heard the sounds of more than one vehicle, the sounds of hammering and chain-sawing, the sounds of cows bawling and men yelling.

Gray and Louise eased past each other in the bath-room doorway, and Gray came to the sink to wash his hands. He brought with him into the room that same sense of the outdoors and hard work that Jill had re-acted to so strongly yesterday.

It was *sexy*. There was just no other way to look at it. The knowledge that he had been out there doing expert, muscular things to corral gates and firewood stacks and truck motors and big, warm animals was just plain, darn sexy. It was something she'd never ex-perienced before.

The smell of engine oil and cow and fresh-cut wood that came from him gave way gradually to the smell of lemony-clean soap. He rinsed his face, wiped it roughly with a towel, then met the reflection of her gaze in the mirror. He froze. The awareness between them zinged like a guitar string wound tight.

"I'll grab that bite," he said, turning from the mir-ror. His voice was as rough as an axe hitting wood.

Jill was still standing in the middle of the bathroom, feeling weak at the knees just thinking about Gray McCall and hammers and nails. He stepped past her, then stopped. His hand came up. His finger touched her face. She felt the brush of his hip against her side.

"You have a piece of oatmeal on your cheek," he said on a low growl.

"Uh…thanks."

"See you down in the yard?"

"Sure." She nodded, and had to stand motionless in the bathroom for a good five minutes after he'd disappeared down the stairs, before her heart stopped hammering.

The electricity between them colored her emotions on the drive into Blue Rock. Sam was dozing against a nest of pillows in the back seat, and she knew it was best if she left him alone. She thought a little more about this station wagon they were riding in, and the fact that it was only last year's model—newer, even, than the attractive modern house that spread out, long and low, on the far hill.

They must have had quite a few good years here, before Gray's dad's death. It would have been confusing and hard to have it turn bad on them so fast, on top of the grief she could see in all of them. Unfortunately, none of them had time for either the confusion or the grief. They were working too hard for that.

And Jill knew from her own experience what this would mean for them as time passed, because she'd been through the same thing herself when her step-dad died. David Brown was the only father she had ever known, and she had loved him, but she'd had to work hard after his death, too.

Rose had pushed her into teaching at the rink, at seventeen, to help pay the bills. She had still been at high school. A year later, she'd been pregnant with Sam. There had been no time for the luxury of grief. This meant that it still hit her sometimes in a powerful, unexpected blast of unresolved feeling that churned inside her like something physical for days until it gradually ebbed again.

Gray braked hard to avoid a bird that had settled briefly in the middle of the road. He swore under his breath.

"Are we going to be late?" Jill asked.

"We're fine."

He just didn't want to be making the trip at all, obviously.

"I hate that this is taking up your morning," she apologized.

"It's not that. I was just…thinking about my dad."

Yeah, and I was thinking about mine….

David Brown had been her true father in every sense that mattered.

"It's the place your thoughts come back to, isn't it?" she said softly.

"All the time, seems like. But it's still not enough. You know, I'm so busy, there's hours go by when I *don't* think about him. And then when I do, when it comes into my mind again, I feel guilty. Like I've let him down. Like I went on vacation and didn't send him a postcard."

"I understand all of that."

He glanced across at her. "Yeah, I guess you do."

It was one of the things they had talked about in Las Vegas, her stepfather's death. Like Franklin McCall, David Brown had had a severe stroke, which had claimed his life just a short time later. In Las Vegas, the things they'd discovered in common had been part of the magic. But now the magic was supposed to dissolve, not go on getting stronger. She hated to think what Alan would say if he knew.

His attitude had been practical, almost hardheaded, from the moment he'd learned of the Las Vegas wedding and the way it had stayed in her mind.

"Of course you can't say yes until you've dealt with it," he'd said. "Go out to Montana and get a glimpse of reality along with the signed divorce papers. Get a glimpse of what this guy's really like when he's not standing under a mirror ball and saving you from a fate worse than death. And maybe you can get some kind of a settlement from him."

"Settlement?"

"Divorce settlement. A payout. Some of those Montana ranchers have a turnover in the millions."

"I don't think he does. Not at the moment."

"Believe me, he can afford it."

"I don't need—"

"But Sam *needs*, Jill. I thought we agreed on that. That our kids come first, whatever it takes. It's why I'm putting my guts into this sales business, to give us all a future. If you can get a settlement from this guy, a nest egg you can invest for Sam, then get one."

She hadn't argued. She'd considered the idea. But she wasn't considering it anymore.

When they reached Blue Rock, Gray carried Sam into the doctor's waiting room, then left them to run his errands. They had a fifteen-minute wait, during which time she read Sam a story and took him to the bathroom.

Dr. Blankenship turned out to be a fearsome looking woman in her forties, wearing a skirt and blouse of brightly patterned silk. But she had a wonderfully soft voice and warm manner, and she wasn't in any doubt about Louise's homemade diagnosis.

"It's the chicken pox, all right! A bad case. He must have had a lot of exposure."

"There were half a dozen kids who came down with it at his pre-school about two and a half weeks ago," Jill said. "But I didn't realize the incubation period was so long. I didn't even think about it until we saw the spots."

"Has he been stressed or run-down at all?"

"He's had a difficult summer," she explained. "We had a fire in our house, while he was in my sister's care. I was in New York for a funeral. That was unsettling for him. More than we realized at first. And more recently, we've been traveling. It was meant to be a kind of a vacation, but now…" She trailed off, then went on, "We're not from around here, obviously. It was good of you to fit us in. We got here from Pennsylvania just yesterday, after a three-day trip and a couple of bad nights."

Dr. Blankenship whistled through her teeth. "That probably didn't help. When are you due to head back?"

Jill made a face. "Due to? This morning. Now… It's your call."

Dr. Blankenship sighed. "Hope this doesn't put a

great big hole in your plans," she said. "But I'd plan to be here at least another ten days, if I were you."

"Ten days…"

"Two or three days until he's not growing anymore spots, and a good week after that to build his energy and his immune system back up. Occasionally, chicken pox can get nasty. I'd like to see him again before you leave, too, to make sure he's up to it. You don't want him coming down with something else on top of this and getting seriously sick."

Jill nodded. "I guess when you put it like that.…"

"You sound pretty reluctant. Is that hard for you? Are you staying with family or friends out here?"

"We're staying with the McCalls. They live on a—"

"Louise and Gray and Louise's dad?" Her severe face lit up. "Why, they've been patients of mine since I started out here, sixteen years ago. They're the best people in the world! Stay three weeks!"

Jill laughed. She didn't explain that it wasn't that easy. She told Gray, "Ten days," when he came to collect her and Sam. She could read in his face all too clearly what he thought about the news. He wasn't any happier about it than she was.

She spent the rest of the day quietly in the house with Sam. The weather was moody and out of sorts. Rain spat from the low sky and the wind cut "as hard as an old maid's tongue," Pete complained.

Jill felt no temptation to follow the other three adults out of doors once lunch was over. They had cattle to move, apparently, from one pasture to another. On horseback. Clearly this was not an operation with which Jill could be of the remotest assistance.

Instead, she put a reluctant Sam in the bath again, and did what work she could around the house later on when he took another nap. His whole body was a miserable mess of watery spots. On his face, she couldn't even find a clear place to kiss him, but kissed him anyway, in his sleep.

Louise and Pete came back to the house just after five, and Jill saw Gray out of her bedroom window, putting the horses away. She recognized Highboy, and knew that the other two were called Cirrus and Madie, but didn't know which was which. The McCalls spoke of them like friends.

She was reading Sam another story when she heard Gray come up the stairs. Sam had always loved books, but he seemed to be clinging to them extra hard at the moment. Something familiar, maybe? Jill loved reading him stories, too. She loved the feel of his warm little body snuggled against her arm, and his dark hair tickling her chin. She loved the sweet sound of his voice as he asked the most unlikely questions.

"Man, that shower is calling me!" she heard Gray say to himself as he came past. She hoped she hadn't used too much hot water in Sam's most recent oatmeal bath.

About ten minutes later Louise called up the stairs, "Dinner's on the table," so Jill hurried to the bathroom to wash up, thinking about what Sam might want to eat. He didn't have much appetite and she didn't know if—

The thought was cut off by her gasp. She'd just collided with a warm and half-naked male torso in the doorway.

"Whoa!" Gray said.

He shot his hands out to steady her, as startled as she was. His hands landed as neat and symmetrical as two shelf brackets right on her hips. They stayed there while she gasped again and flattened a palm against her chest. The palm rested just above the twin swells of her breasts and drew his attention to the way her chest rose as she took a huge gulp of air.

"Gray, I didn't realize you were still in there!"

"Uh, well, I'm almost not," he answered. "I mean, I was on my way out."

Someone give the man a prize for stating the obvious! he thought in disgust.

Then he wondered uneasily just how far up he'd bothered to zip his jeans a moment ago. Far enough to keep them hanging on his hips until he reached a clean shirt in his bedroom under normal circumstances. But holding onto a wide-eyed Jill Brown while he was in a state of semi-nakedness *wasn't* a normal circumstance.

In fact, it was such a very unusual circumstance that his body wasn't about to waste the opportunity. It…bits of it…reacted straight away. His hands, instead of dropping to his sides, slid further around to where they could fully appreciate the exact way her rear end so snugly filled her jeans.

His feet, instead of stepping to the side, stepped forward then quickly shuffled back again. He realized his jeans definitely weren't going to stay up, and that when they dropped, the most dramatic reaction of all would become startlingly apparent to her.

"Your mom said dinner's on the table, did you

hear?'' she said, just as he finally let go of her and hauled up the waistband of his Wranglers instead.

Just in time.

By sucking in his lower stomach to a painful degree, he managed to get the fly done up, then twisted the metal button through the hole with fingers that shook slightly. Fingers that would much have preferred to be unfastening buttons than fastening them up, he knew.

Her buttons.

The mauve ones that marched in a straight line from the V neck of her close-fitting cardigan sweater, between her softly swelling breasts and all the way down to her waist.

"Yes, I heard," he said, and managed to get past her at last to the safety and solitude of his bedroom.

Ten days, he thought as he hauled on his shirt. Lord, he was still shaking! He groaned. She's going to be here for another ten days!

Ten more days of him and Jill rubbing up against each other, the way two people inevitably did when they shared the same space. Ten more days of hearing the water in the shower, and knowing she was the one standing under it, lathering soap all over her silky skin. Ten more days of bumping into her in doorways, of watching the way she ate and the way she laughed and the way she so tenderly kissed and hugged her son.

Ten days of knowing that her bedroom shared a wall with his, and that her underwear tangled with his in the dryer, of knowing that he'd see her when he walked in the kitchen door at the end of the day, and minutes after he pulled his boots on each morning.

"This'd be a whole lot easier if we weren't married," he muttered aloud in his room.

Then he laughed and shook his head. Crazy! If they weren't married, she wouldn't be here, so it didn't make sense.

That didn't stop it from being true.

There was something about being married. He kept thinking about what marriage meant. It meant sharing. Sharing your space as he was doing with Jill. Sharing your stories. They had begun to do that, too, the very first night they met. Sharing your lives...

And marriage meant one more thing, too. It meant sharing a bed.

This was where his body parted company from his brain. His brain might be able to say, "Not now. Not yet. There'll come a time when you can go looking for the right woman to share your life with. A woman who doesn't have a child, because you've run out on that kind of a relationship twice already, not to mention witnessing just how ugly it got between Dad and Mitch."

But all his body could tell him was, "There's a woman here right now. So what if there's Sam, too? You want Jill. And you're married to her. And married people can do what they want in that department, so why the heck don't you just go for it?"

He groaned again.

Ten more days...

"Can you read to me some more, Mommy?" Sam said after dinner.

"You're not sleepy yet?"

"I slept all day."

Not quite true, but true enough. Jill suspected that it wouldn't be helpful to put him to bed now. In any case, she had a good reason for wanting him to stay up. Louise had taken Pete into town to visit a sick friend, leaving Jill and Gray the only adults in the house. One small, sick child to act as chaperone was better than no chaperone at all.

"I'll read to you, Sam," she said. "But it'll have to be the stories we've already read."

She had brought half a dozen of his favorite books with them to help entertain him on the train journey, but they must have read each of those three times on the trip so far.

"We have some kids' books in a box somewhere," Gray said. "I remember packing them when we moved out of the new house. They were books I had when I was little."

Sam's droopy, red-rimmed eyes lit up a little. "New stories? That would be great! Do you do voices?"

"Voices?"

"Mommy does funny voices in stories. Do you?"

"Honey, I don't think Gray meant that *he* was going to read you the stories," Jill said.

"No? Okay, you then, Mommy."

"I'll go hunt up the box," Gray came in quickly, and Jill saw the relief on his face.

He was awkward with Sam. She noticed it frequently. He was distant. Uncomfortable. Asked the right questions about how Sam was feeling, but that was about it. Hadn't begun to build a relationship with him the way Louise was doing so easily.

Jill told herself that there was no reason to feel disappointed about it. It was part of the "reality" that Alan had talked about back home. The reality of what this rancher rescuer of hers was really like, away from the Las Vegas lights. He didn't put kids first, apparently, the way Alan did.

I have to call Alan and tell him what's going on, she thought. *He was hoping to meet us in Chicago in a few days.*

She asked Gray if she could make the call, just as he was about to disappear upstairs, and he nodded. "Of course. Use my office."

Like the other rooms in the house, it was filled with boxes still packed after the move down from the main house. Jill didn't take much notice of them, just got on the phone and made her call.

"I couldn't have made Chicago this week, anyhow," Alan told her. It was meant to console her, but instead it only added to a sense of distance that she wasn't happy about. "Can't take the time from the business. There's a chance of a big sale coming through."

He wanted to know how the divorce thing was going. Was McCall making any trouble? Or any offers?

"Have you asked him about a settlement yet?"

"No, I haven't asked him about a settlement yet," she echoed, her voice heavy with dissatisfaction at the way this conversation was going.

She heard a sound behind her, and Gray stood in the doorway. He'd heard her last words. His face left her in no doubt of that. His eyes were steady and dark, and his mouth narrow and straight. He didn't say anything.

He didn't need to. Neither did she. After all, did it matter if he thought she had a mercenary streak?

"But you will, won't you?" she heard down the line.

"I don't know," she told Alan, fobbing him off. She didn't want to argue the point. Not now.

"The box of books is in here," Gray said. "I remember seeing it the other day."

He stepped across the room, and sure enough, there it was, marked like the other boxes in black felt-tip pen. He hefted it up and took it out of the room, and she ended the phone call to Alan fifteen minutes later, having spent longer on it than she wanted to. Sam would be impatient by now, waiting for her.

But when she reached the living room, he wasn't. He hadn't needed to. Gray was reading to him instead. Reluctantly? If so, he seemed to have gotten over that for the moment.

They sat together on the old, quilt-covered couch. Gray's voice was slow and low, and the words were poetry. Children's classics from a big book full of whimsical illustrations. He said each line carefully, as if he was really thinking about it, and he read beautifully, the rough edges of his workday cowboy's voice smoothed into music.

"I will make you brooches and toys for your delight
Of bird-song at morning and star-shine at night."

Just one problem. Sam wasn't listening anymore. He was asleep.

Gray hadn't noticed yet. Sam's head was still rest-

ing in the crook of his arm, lolled just slightly forward.
Jill couldn't bear to interrupt just yet. He came to the
last lines of the verse.

"I will make a palace fit for you and me
Of green days in forests and blue days at sea."

Then he looked up at Jill and smiled, slightly self-
conscious, and she pointed to Sam's closed eyes and
said, "Thanks."

"Wh—?" He craned his head a little and saw what
had happened. He gave a crooked grin. "Guess Robert
Louis Stevenson and I bored him into it."

"You lulled him," she corrected. "You must have
had his full attention, or he wouldn't have sat still long
enough to let it happen."

"I like kids' poetry," he said. "I loved this book
when I was a kid. I used to imagine all the heroes were
me. Till I hit my teens and got this bee in my bonnet
about bronc-riding."

"You wanted to be a rodeo rider?" Not a subject
she knew anything about.

"For a few years. Till I realized how much travel
was involved, when I'd rather have been here working
the ranch. Long enough, though, to have some pretty
spectacular falls."

"Oh, I know about falls."

"You do?"

"From skating. You think dirt is hard, you should
try falling on solid ice, then getting up straight away
to go into a lay-back spin with a smile on your face."

"I guess there are some similarities," he agreed.

Neither of them wanted to pursue the idea. She wasn't here to look for similarities between them, of any kind.

"Thanks for reading to him," she said quickly.

"It was nothing." His voice had roughened. She'd have sworn he'd enjoyed reading to Sam, but now he seemed to be rejecting those moments. "You... uh...needed to finish your call," he added.

The words he'd overhead her saying to Alan hung in the air between them.

She gabbled, "I'm not planning to try and get a financial settlement out of you, Gray. You don't have to worry about that."

"Wouldn't do you much good if you were," he answered. "I can't afford to give you one. You've probably realized that."

Which is the only reason you wouldn't bother to ask, his tone implied.

Reality, again.

"Do you want to get Sam up to bed?"

"We should," she agreed.

But the old couch was low and soft, and he and Sam were sunk right down into it.

"I'm not going to be able to shift and get to my feet without disturbing him," Gray decided.

"He'll probably wake anyway if it's anyone but me carrying him up the stairs."

"You'd better take him, then. I'll help as much as I can."

He eased himself a little straighter, but Jill had to bend low over him, all the same. Sam was pillowed against his left arm. Jill slid her left arm between their two bodies, feeling the hard warmth of Gray's chest and the softness of his shirt.

Her other arm came around to meet the first one in the middle of Sam's back, but then she realized she wasn't going to be able to do it like that. Her left arm needed to be lower. Much lower. Under Sam's thighs.

And since her head was already very close to Gray's…in fact her forehead was pressing into his neck…she could see the way the muscles in his jaw tightened as her forearm slid down his body.

She felt the rise and fall of his careful breathing. She smelled soap and beer and clean shirt. Her knuckles grazed his hip. Her elbow bumped against something else that was hard and might have been…*must* have been…his other hip. It certainly wasn't his belt buckle.

"Got him," she said. "Sorry. Sit still. I'm just—" With a grunt of effort she lifted up her child and buried her face in his hair. He had chicken pox on his scalp.

Gray had something in his throat. It made his voice husky. "When you get back down," he said, "I'll make coffee and put on a movie. Okay?"

"Okay," she nodded. Her cheeks were hot.

"Did he stay asleep?"

"So far."

"He's not going to be too heavy?"

"No. I'm used to it."

"Good."

"I'll be down in a minute," she said, and escaped up the stairs.

Chapter Five

"Hey, cowboy, you're feeling better!" Louise McCall said to Sam when he came down to a late breakfast three days later.

"Yup," he answered, then added in a hopeful tone, after a quarter second's pause, "Is there pancakes, like yesterday?"

His appetite had returned when he awoke the previous morning, though he'd still been lacking in energy. Today he obviously had energy as well.

"Sorry, not today," Louise said. "There's eggs, or oatmeal…"

"How about just cereal, honey," Jill cut in.

Everyone else's breakfast was long cleared away, and Louise was busy cutting a large stack of sandwiches, parcelling up slices of cake and adding boiling water to two big thermos flasks. Sam observed these preparations and interpreted them in his own way.

"Hey, are we going on a picnic?"

"No, honey—" Jill began.

But Louise answered, "Kind of. We have a big section of fence to check and fix, and we don't want to have to come back for lunch."

"And are we coming, too?"

Sam's face lit up. It was totally covered in crusted-over spots, as was pretty much the entire rest of his body, including several places that Jill didn't want to think about. Who ever heard of chicken pox on your tongue? She had bathed him in oatmeal starch nine times over the past three days, according to Louise's time-honored wisdom, and as Louise had promised, that had kept him from scratching.

Now the old spots had crusted over and no new ones were coming. He wasn't infectious anymore and he clearly felt almost like his usual self. This gave Jill the breathing space to fully realize just how much of a nuisance the two of them had been over the past few days.

Oh, she'd done her best to be useful. She'd washed dishes, put laundry in the drier, passed the vacuum cleaner. But she wasn't fooling herself. It wasn't enough to make up for the trouble they'd caused, and Gray didn't always manage to hide the fact.

Louise had taken Sam's meals up to him on a tray both days. Gray had read him more bedtime stories and poems last night. As before, his voice was like gentle, rough-hewn music, and Sam had hung on every word. Clearly, he liked the man, but Jill wasn't convinced that the feeling was mutual.

"That's up to your mom, Sam," Louise was saying. "We don't want to get in the way."

Louise stopped what she was doing, put her hands on her hips and frowned.

"Now, how could you do that?" she demanded. "This is a big, open ranch we're talking about, here, not some poky office. And Dr. Blankenship says you're here for at least another week. What are you going to do with yourselves if you just stay in the house? Of course you can come, if you want to. I was going to suggest it, and I've cut enough sandwiches."

Jill was silent for a moment. It had to be a sincere offer, didn't it? She'd been relieved at the way the life of the ranch had gone on as usual since their arrival. It lessened her indebtedness, and her sense of intrusion. But there were several times when she'd seen Gray or his mother going out of their way for her.

"I won't work in the office tonight," Gray had said each evening, gruff and casual. "Think I'll catch a movie instead."

He'd invited Jill to choose from a pile of home-recorded tapes. Then he had brought in coffee and cookies and sprawled onto the couch as if he simply couldn't think of a better way to spend an evening. Jill felt like an idiot, on the third evening, half way through *Groundhog Day*, because it had only just occurred to her that he was doing this for her benefit. In reality, he was probably itching to get onto his computer and examine spreadsheets and bovine growth charts and whatever.

Too late to say anything. Far too late to admit how much she'd enjoyed the quiet evenings. His honest laugh. His courteous inquiries of, "More coffee, Jill?" Her burning sense of his body just inches from hers on

the long couch, while Louise worked quietly on her
patchwork piecing in a nearby armchair, glancing up
occasionally at the TV screen.

Jill could practically hear Gray's muscles letting go
after his hard, physical day. Twice he dozed off and
ended up with his head on her shoulder and his thigh
stretched against hers. Both times, she didn't inch away
nearly as quickly as she should have.

So, did she risk any similar intrusion on Gray's plans
by accepting Louise's offer today? And did she risk
anything else?

She was spending too much time in Gray's company
already. The most able-bodied and vigorous people in
the house, they were first up in the mornings and last
to bed at night, which meant they had quiet times together when they could talk. Times they could have
fallen into each other's arms and kissed hungrily if
they'd let themselves.

Jill had lost count of the times they'd come close to
doing just that. Breakfast that first day, before she'd
known that Sam had the chicken pox, when they had
both been thinking back on a Las Vegas dawn. Before
dinner that same night, when she'd met his half-naked,
muscular torso in the bathroom doorway...

It would be easier and far safer to say no to the
picnic. But then she saw Sam's eyes full of eager, silent
pleading, and made her decision.

"Okay, sure, we'll come, as long as you let me
help."

She soon regretted that last naive offer.

The battered pickup that Gray had been working on
the other day wheeled to a halt in front of the house.

Louise had the picnic supplies ready, so Jill and Sam helped carry them out.

"Got a hat and a jacket and a change of clothes for Sam?" the older woman asked.

This sent Jill hurrying back inside and up the stairs, cursing her own lack of preparation. When she came back out, Gray's grandfather was sitting on a pile of old grain bags in the back of the vehicle, while Louise was at the wheel and Gray himself was waiting by the passenger door.

Just the sight of the equipment in the back of the truck convinced Jill at once that she would be about as much help in keeping two pieces of uncooperative fence together as would a plastic hair clip. There were coils of wire strung with sharp, ugly barbs, a hammer and a couple of boxes of huge nails, steel posts, shovels, a chain saw and several tools she'd never seen before. Some kind of pry bar, some kind of pliers, various staples and clips, also packed in boxes.

Sam was seated up front next to Louise, so Jill went to climb into the back next to Grandpa Pete, till Gray growled, "You're in front, Jill," and held the door open for her.

"Oh, but I thought…"

"I figure my tailbone's harder than yours," he said. "It's going to be a bumpy ride."

She nodded and didn't argue, torn in two once more by a familiar dilemma. Was she more of a nuisance when she went along with what Gray's innate courtesy led him to suggest? Or when she argued back?

He shut the door for her, then warned, "Handle doesn't work on the inside. You have to wind the win-

dow down and do it from the outside, or wait until I
let you out.''

He climbed in the back, and Louise started off. They
drove for ten minutes on tracks that Jill considered in-
sanely rough, then veered suddenly onto a piece of
ground where there wasn't any track at all. Spotty Sam
shrieked with excitement and laughter at every bounce,
while Louise stared ahead in ferocious, narrow-eyed
concentration. Her hands looked like they were welded
to the steering wheel, and she avoided tree stumps and
rocks and ditches with quick-thinking and violent
wrenches of her arms.

With the window wide open and one elbow stuck
out of it into the fresh air, Jill was grinning one minute
and closing her eyes in terror the next. Gray twisted
around on his grain bags and yelled to her, ''Everything okay up front?''

And she yelled back, ''Yes!'' before she even
stopped to think about it.

They went over a terrific bump and she came down
hard on her tailbone, but somehow it didn't matter.
Despite the bumps and the dust and the jolts of terror,
she was loving this. Dew still shone on the straw-
colored grass in some spots. A fresh, mild breeze
kicked at the flaming leaves or the tufted needles of
trees whose names she didn't know. She'd never been
in a place this wild, never set out on an expedition with
this sort of hard work at the end of it, and it was ex-
hilarating.

Suddenly, after five minutes, Louise stopped and announced, ''Okay, this is the difficult bit coming up
now.''

Jill choked. "Uh...what have we just been driving on, then?"

"The less difficult bit," Louise answered with a grin. "Which I can handle. But Gray can get the truck over the last two hundred yards."

"Should I...get in back, then?"

"Nope. If you've got any sense, you and Sam will do what I'm going to do, and walk!"

She hopped out, far too nimble for a woman in her fifties, and said, "All yours, Gray."

"This is where we get out, sweetie," Jill told her son.

She went to open the door, but the handle wobbled in her hand and Gray came and did it for her, from the outside.

"Excuse my cursing," he said.

"You haven't been cursing."

She slid off the high seat of the pickup and onto the ground. The movement brought her up against his thigh for a moment and she was swamped in his male aura of strength and musk and warm fabric. He stiffened, and her breathing went shallow.

Again. Why did it keep happening, when neither of them wanted it?

She fought back a shuddering sigh.

"That's a warning, not an apology," he said, stepping quickly back and turning his head away. Why was the hood of the trunk suddenly such a fascinating object for him? "You're going to hear the cursing in a minute," he added.

"Oh. Right."

Grandpa Pete got out to walk, too. They let Gray get

a head start, then followed along, watching him work
the vehicle. Several short, yelled exclamations that Jill
couldn't understand floated through the window. Gray
had, however, left her in little doubt about their general
content. At least six times she was sure the truck was
going to topple or slide or balk. Twice he scraped the
chassis across bare rock, and once he splintered a half-
rotted tree trunk as he ground the wheels over it.

Finally, he fetched up beneath a crooked tree, at an
angle that had Jill expecting all the equipment to come
sliding right out the back as soon as he lowered the
tailgate.

"It's a big section," Gray's grandfather commented
in his laconic way as he studied the terrain just ahead.

"All across the creek and beyond the corner post,"
Gray agreed, coming to stand beside him. "And we
should check it a good ways along in both directions."

Jill realized they were talking about the downed
fence. She could see it now, lying flat across the wide,
partially dry bed of the creek. It was completely broken
in some parts, the strands of wire tangled and rusted
and useless. In other places, it was thickly felted with
debris from the floods of spring snowmelt several
months ago.

"And there's three more of our cows, across into
Thurrell Creek," Louise said. "No, make that five.
Want to come and help me chase 'em back, Sam?"

"Yeah?" he said, as if she might have been teasing.

"Yeah," she confirmed. "It's fun." To Jill, she
added, "Maddening, but fun." Then to Sam again,
"Come on, cowboy."

She clapped an old straw cowboy hat on his head

and the two of them strode off. Jill watched them and had to hide a grin which contained a twist of pain that she didn't quite understand.

Just look at him! Four years old, and not big for his age. His cowboy stride was about twice as long as his little legs could handle, but he kept it up for a good twenty paces before he lapsed into a skippetty-hop of a run to keep up with Louise. He had the hat pushed back on his head, and his shoulders set like a U.S. marine, square and serious. He was all set to do this, to throw himself into it, and to love it, showing an eagerness she'd never seen in him before.

It made her wonder how happy he had truly been with his life before this.

She'd never actually asked. How did you ask a kid something like that? "Are you happy, Sam?"

What was so different about this place? What had caught at his spirit so strongly, despite his illness?

Was it the openness and grandeur of the landscape? Or was it the wild, changeable weather? They had been flung back into Indian summer, now, with sunny skies and cotton-ball clouds after there had been substantial snowfalls on the higher peaks at the beginning of the week as well as sleet in the McCalls' own yard.

Or maybe it was the animals and the work of the ranch? Sam had been well enough to go out to the barn with Gray for a short spell, yesterday afternoon. He treated it like an adventure and came back with more information about sick cows than Jill could keep in her head for more than five minutes.

Without an answer to her questions, she put them aside and turned to Gray. He was helping his grandfather unload equipment from the back of the truck. "What can I do?"

"Pour me a coffee while I take a look at this project?" he suggested.

She nodded, then watched as he strode off along the bank of the creek, assessing which sections of fence needed repair and which needed complete replacement. The sun shone on his hat and on his broad back, he had his shirt sleeves rolled, and that stride of his was—

Sam's. It was Sam's. That stride was what Sam had been imitating as he walked off with Louise.

Jill had her answer, now. *This* was the difference. This was the thing that a ranch in Montana possessed, and the thing that a big, old Victorian house in Pennsylvania completely lacked. A man. A big, strong, capable, honorable, fine figure of a man whom Sam could look up to and imitate and respect.

Sam had never known his father. Curtis Harrington III had got himself out of Jill's life with indecent haste the moment he'd learned that she was pregnant. What he was doing now, she had no idea. Cared even less, after so long. At least, she didn't care about the man himself. She cared a whole lot for the idea of a good father for Sam, and that was why she was going to say yes to Alan.

As soon as her divorce from Grayson McCall was through.

To give Sam a man in his life whom he could respect. A decent provider, a man who had duties and responsibilities and who took every one of them seriously. Not a man that used the word "love." Not a man who made her pulses flutter and her head go giddy.

No, thanks. She'd had that with Curtis for a whole three months. She'd discovered the hard way that it didn't mean squat, because it didn't last, that stuff about love, and it blinded you to who a man truly was.

She had responded to Alan Jennings because he *didn't* do any of that crazy stuff to her. He didn't quicken her pulse by so much as a beat. Didn't make her double up in shared laughter, or get a glow in her cheeks when she caught his gaze, or make her eyes light up when they discovered a taste or an opinion or a past experience that they shared.

But she liked him. She liked his confident, hard-edged ideas on life, now that she'd turned her back on those foolish showgirl dreams of hers. She liked his constant focus on their kids and on building security. It was a better basis for a marriage than the black magic of chemistry any day.

Couldn't you have both? Her sisters had each challenged her with that question.

She didn't think so, and she was gambling her whole future on this decision. Her future and Sam's. Alan liked Sam. He worried about him a lot. Shouldn't he have learned to tie his shoelaces by now? Wasn't he small for his age? Was that little cut on his finger in danger of getting infected?

Attention to detail, Alan called it, and it was how he planned to build his business up, he said. Jill couldn't fault him for any of it. Sam seemed to like Alan. Certainly didn't dislike him, and Alan always tried very hard. But it occurred to her, now, that Sam had never treated Alan as a role model or a companion in any way. Suddenly, that seemed like a problem, despite all the pluses she kept listing to herself.

"Coffee? Great!" Gray said. "Thanks, Jill."

His black eyes flashed into hers for a moment, and she felt a stab of need deep within her that was frightening. Darn it, hadn't she just finished reminding herself about the fact that she wasn't looking for any of those raw, physical feelings? Hadn't she spent four days fighting them with everything she had?

She didn't want them.

"You're welcome, Gray," she answered him, deliberately moving away from the dangerous radiance of his body heat.

He gulped the coffee scalding hot, then spent three hours teaching her about fence.

"Hard work" didn't begin to cut it. She got three long gashes on her arm from the wicked barbs in the wire. Got blisters from gripping the fence stretcher. Got a ring of dusty sweat around her neck and aching muscles from trying to pound posts until Gray gave up getting her to do that part, even in the softer soil beside the creek bed, and took turns at it with Grandpa Pete instead.

"You can stop," Gray told her more than once.

But she just glared at him and eventually he got the message. "You don't give up on things, do you?"

"It's called seeing it through," she answered. "And it's supposed to teach me not to jump into these kinds of things so fast, but it never works. Besides, I'm having fun."

"Yeah...?"

She hardly had time to think about Sam or Louise, who had brought their five mama cows back across onto McCall land and gone in search of four more they'd seen farther off. There was no doubt that Sam was enjoying himself. Every now and then she could hear his high treble voice yelling exotic incantations as if they were his native language.

"Come on, mama, hike out. Hike around, there. Hoi! Hoi! Step up, there! Step up there, mama!"

Gray heard him, too, and paused in his post pounding long enough to say, with his usual wry grin, "He's doing a good job, there, Jill." His attitude toward Sam seemed just a little less stiff and reluctant than it had a couple of days ago.

"I think your mom's doing most of the work," she answered. "And all of the strategy."

"But he's yelling when she tells him to and staying quiet at the right times, too," he pointed out. "Isn't always easy to get cows to go where you want 'em to, especially when you're not on horseback. This section of fence was Stannard's responsibility, and it's been down since we bought the place, without us knowing it. That's part of the problem. These cows have gotten used to crossing onto Thurrell Creek with nothing getting in their way."

"But why does that matter? The land's yours, now."

"Yes, but it isn't in great shape. I tried to rent it out in spring, but couldn't get anyone to take it on for a short-term lease. It needs too much work. Parts have been overstocked, and a lot of it has been neglected. There's barbed wire down that the cattle could gash themselves on, weeds we don't want spread and don't want them to feed on." He reached into a gnarled bush a couple of feet away and pulled a long piece of orange nylon string out of the scratchy branches. "And see this?"

"Uh-huh," she nodded.

"This isn't ours. It blew over from Thurrell Creek. We collect up every piece of string from our feed bales, because they can do horrible things to cattle when they're left loose."

Jill shuddered, and nodded again, not wanting to think too hard about what those horrible things might be.

"There'll be more of them on the other property. I don't want to run cattle on the place until I get a better chance to see which parts are in good enough shape. That would have been Dad's plan, too."

He checked the depth of the new steel post he was putting in, then pounded it a little harder, until he was satisfied. Jill had her own task, meanwhile—sharpening the teeth on the chain saw with a cylindrical file.

Gray had used the chain saw several times already to cut through deadfall that was in the way of the fence line. His muscles worked easily beneath his shirt, and his stance was as solid as a tree trunk. As soon as he was done with this post, they moved onto the next one. He went on talking as he worked.

"Ties me in knots when I think about that ranch," he said. Seemed he needed to talk out his feelings aloud, as if they'd been pent up inside him for too long. "Place used to belong to the Thurrell family. You met Ron."

"The garage owner."

"That's the one. And there's his sister C.J. and her husband who run the motel."

"The one that was no good for Sam when he was sick?"

Gray nodded. "The Sagebrush. Ron and C.J.'s dad lost the ranch to Wylie Stannard on a bet, but his kids can't let go of the idea of the place. They wanted it back, but Dad beat the price they came up with. They weren't happy. They've made me a couple of offers, but I'm not selling." His jaw jutted stubbornly. "Dad wanted the place, and he was right to take it, despite the way we're stretched. I'll make it work, somehow, the way Dad must have planned. Once we can lick it into shape, we'll have a beautiful spread, together with Flaming Hills."

His black eyes took a sweeping look out over his own land and the new holding, and he leaned on the half-pounded steel post for a moment. Jill's breath caught in her chest as she watched him. She forgot about filing the saw's jagged teeth.

Lord, he loved this ranch! He loved it, she sensed, in a way he never put into words. This kind of love was about hard work, clear-eyed understanding and unspoken satisfaction. About a deep vein of fear, too, that he would fail and thereby let his beloved father down. Had Frank misjudged the purchase of the new ranch? Or was it Gray who was making mistakes? Hard to see it that way.

"Trouble with the Thurrells," he went on, "their Dad was never much good at ranching, and from the way Ron and C.J. run their current business operations, there's no reason to think they'd be any better."

"Yeah, I wasn't too impressed with Ron's garage or his car."

"You can't get away with cheating land and cattle the way you can sometimes get away with cheating people. They'd run the place down even worse than it is already, if they ever got hold of it. Which would be a cryin' shame, because the Thurrell Creek ranch could be a beautiful piece of land, if it was worked right. Good water and pasture, none of it too exposed." He went on, speaking almost to himself, "Maybe that's why Dad was prepared to stretch us so thin. He couldn't stand to see the place in the wrong hands."

She nodded again and wanted to say something. Something that would let him know she understood. Nothing came, and before her brain could get itself going properly, he'd added, "How's that saw coming?"

"Fine. I must be back to the beginning of the teeth by now."

"Want to learn how to use it?"

No, thanks. I'm only here for another week, if Sam keeps on feeling this good. It's not a skill I'll have a lot of use for in the future.

That would have been the sensible thing to say. Yup. Definitely.

Instead, what came out of her mouth was a perky yet determined, "Sure!"

Insane. Impulsive. As usual.

Then she remembered what her stepfather used to say. "If someone gives you the chance to learn something new, take it. You never know when you may need it.'' Had David Brown been thinking of chain saws? Doubtful. She sensed he'd approve, though.

He would have approved of Gray, too….

Gray started the chain saw. It rattled then screamed, kicking in his strong, smoothly muscled hands. He showed her how to hold on to it, where the kill switch was, how to let it bite and how to safely pull it free of the newly made cut. It wasn't a piece of equipment that you could love, but the results were satisfying.

Within fifteen minutes, she had cut through several trunks of deadfall. Once the manic implement threatened to jump out of her hands, and she had to use the kill switch fast. But on the whole she didn't think she'd done too badly. She got her reward when Louise and Sam showed up and Louise decreed it was time for lunch.

''Cows are scared of me, Mom,'' Sam reported proudly, when Jill had killed the sound of the saw.

''Maybe it's the spots on your face,'' she teased her son.

''He did a good job,'' Louise reported. ''And so have you, Jill.''

''Oh…thanks.''

Once again, she didn't know what to say. She didn't want to betray how pleased she was at Louise's observation. Could you call it a compliment? Why did it give her such a kick of pleasure to be told she'd done well at tasks no self-respecting city girl would want to tackle even once, let alone for a second time?

She was afraid to think about the answer to this question.

It was a relief to contemplate Louise's hearty sandwiches and thick wedges of orange butter cake instead. First she poured some ice water for Sam, gulped some herself, then poured fresh cups of the coffee that was still piping hot, for each of the adults. Louise honked the horn of the pickup, which brought Grandpa Pete out of the scrubby trees on the far side of the creek.

He'd been patrolling a section of fence that was basically intact but had the occasional strand of broken wire or rotted wooden post which needed replacing with steel. As usual, he didn't say much, just ate and drank slowly, watching the water run in the creek. Sam finished eating first and asked if he could play in the water.

Louise and Jill looked at each other for confirmation, and Jill told him, "Yes, because we have spare clothing for you, if you get wet." She added hastily, "Not that that's a suggestion to go swimming, honey. You don't want to get sick again."

"Shoot," Gray said. "There's some more cows I've just spotted over on Thurrell Creek. Want to see if you're as good as your son is at scaring 'em back, Jill?"

"Go on, Mom," Sam said. "It's fun."

So Jill followed Gray, chewing on her butter cake as she went, just as he was doing.

Lord, but the man moved well! Fast and nimble over the rough terrain, despite his impressive size. Jill struggled to keep up, until he noticed and waited for her. His black eyes were hard to read as he watched her progress.

She didn't want to think too much about the way he affected her. Anyway, maybe it wasn't him but this country of his that was making her senses so alive today. She felt dizzy with the freshness of the air and the dazzle of the sun, the smell of water and dust and grass, the sound of birds and wind singing through wire.

It couldn't just be Gray. Or was he so much a part of his land that you couldn't tell the two feelings apart?

"Why did Wylie let his ranch run down like that?" she asked. She needed the distraction of words.

Not that Gray's gruff, careful voice was a whole lot easier to take than the sight of his strong body. They were walking side by side, now. She could tell he was matching his pace to hers, but he didn't show any impatience about it.

"He wasn't working it himself, the past few years," Gray answered her. "He was getting too old, and his two sons had moved back east. They weren't interested in ranching. He moved in with the elder one a few years back, and leased out the place. Wish he'd sold it to Dad straight off, before we put the money into the new house. We'd have had the capital we needed, then. Place wouldn't have required so much time and money put into it, as well. Still..." Gray frowned suddenly, took his hat off his head in a frustrated gesture, crushed its felt crown in his hands, then put it back on again. "No use thinking that way."

"But you sold cattle just a couple of weeks ago, right? Where did that money go?"

"It's mostly put aside to service the loan for the next year, and for handling day to day costs," Gray explained in his usual careful way.

"Okay," Jill answered. His way of talking warmed

her. He spoke as if it was important that he explained it right, important that she understood.

"If we get a good drop of calves next season, and don't lose too many mamas over winter," he went on, "we should do a little better. Have enough cash to start building the breeding herd back up, get some of the machinery back in shape. But it's going to be tight. Real tight. We don't have the manpower to go out constantly checking for sick animals, or calves that drop in the middle of a late blizzard. We're going to lose some."

"When did you let go of the hands?"

"The last of them, round about the time I got your letter." His mouth hardly moved on the words. "Dacey Lenart had been on this ranch fifteen years."

"Gray, I'm sorry, I'm asking all these questions, making you talk about it."

"It's okay. These are facts. Talking about 'em's not going to make 'em any worse. Or make 'em go away, worse luck! I…uh…appreciate your interest," he finished in his courteous way.

She couldn't reply. Her sense of how much all this hurt him was like a punch in the stomach, and she found she'd instinctively folded her hands there to cradle the ache away.

Over the past few days, she'd tried so hard not to think about the fact that she and Gray were husband and wife. She tried to focus on leaving in a week, without a backward glance. But the thought of a man like Gray struggling so hard, dragging his good-hearted, hard-working mother and grandfather down with him, was hard to bear.

"There are the cattle," Gray said. "In that stand of pines. They're not going to be easy to get out and get headed in the right direction. It spooks 'em to have people coming at 'em on foot."

He wasn't wrong.

The three four-footed female beasts led the two two-legged creatures on a roguish chase that lasted a good twenty minutes before they finally headed at a decisive canter in completely the wrong direction. Jill was hot and damp and out of breath. She had pine needles down her shirt and a scratch on her face, and she had more swear words running in her head than she'd said out loud in her whole life.

Gray was less inhibited. He had to be making half those curse-words up on the spot, but they were pretty effective, all the same. Jill knew he'd have gone with the original versions if she wasn't within earshot. He was a gentleman that way, and she liked it. Too much.

"Those d…danged, f…frog-gone animals are not going to stop until they get to the next belt of trees," he predicted in frustration, and he was right.

They stood together and watched it happen, at which point Jill sank down on the soft carpet of cinnamon-colored pine needles and howled at her powerlessness.

"Gray, I hate to say this, but your fifty-some-year-old mother and my four-year-old son were a lot better at this than we are."

"You think so?"

"We've just proved it, haven't we?"

With a groan and a laugh, she rolled onto her back and looked up through the radiating branches of the trees to glimpses of blue sky. The pines soughed in the breeze, and the needles—no doubt tangling in her hair at this very moment—were like a fragrant pillow.

"I prefer to theorize that the difference is in the cows," Gray answered solemnly.

He dropped down beside her, almost as breathless, and settled on his back, too. For a stretched out moment, they lay side by side in the quiet stillness of the woods. His shirt sleeve touched her bare arm, just below her pale blue T-shirt.

"These are yearlings," he said, "and they're a lot friskier and less set in their ways."

"Frisky... Remind me, what does that word mean? I don't think I can move another step."

"You're going to have to, Jill," he said, without mercy.

He was back on his feet already, and he reached down, grabbed her hand and hauled her up. She went clumsily and lurched against him. A second later, her breathlessness was back, only this time it couldn't be blamed on the cows.

Gray hadn't let go of her hand. He should have. She was steady now. But he hadn't. Instead, he had his fingers laced through hers, brushing her thigh, and she could feel the hard, brown warmth of his forearm against hers. He was very still.

For a timeless interval of silence, she stared at his chest, mesmerized by the steady rise and fall of his breathing, and by the V of smooth skin that disappeared into his shirt. Then she raised her head and saw at once in his eyes that he was going to kiss her. They were dark and wide and almost startled, below the shadow of his felt hat, as if what he was feeling had shocked him.

Not much of a surprise, this. It had shocked her. Was still shocking her. All those times in the confinement of the house when they'd managed to resist each other. Managed to deny the magic. Now, with a whole ranch around them and a whole Montana sky overhead, they couldn't deny the magic anymore.

Her lower lip trembled as she waited for the touch of his mouth, and when it came she felt a shudder of need ripple through her. He brushed the corner of her mouth with closed lips, the feather-light touch more tantalizing than a full kiss could have been.

A little sound escaped from her throat and she raised her face higher, closed her eyes. His fingers found her other hand and held it. His lips parted, clung, drifted and clung again. They were lazy about it at first, the way they might lazily have sipped at a cool drink on a summer's day. Taste and brush. Draw in a little breath, press and nibble and tangle with lips and teeth and tongue.

Then it grew hungrier, deeper and more urgent. Jill felt her head loll, then arch back. She had to gasp for air because she was drowning in his mouth, drowning in the taste of him. There was a fire licking low in her belly. She felt his eyelashes brush her cheek and the muscles in his forearm twitch and harden as he went on gripping her hands.

He groaned. "You smell so good," he breathed.

Desperately, she grabbed for some humor, like a shipwrecked sailor grabbing for a rock in a churning sea.

"Yeah, sure, like the 'before' segment in an anti-perspirant commercial." The words were blurred and broken by his mouth.

"No, like pine needles…" he said.

"So do you, Grayson McCall," she muttered, and gave up the fight.

Chapter Six

Grayson James McCall was a man who kissed with his eyes closed.

He always had been. From the shy peck he'd landed on his playmate Gloria's cheek back in kindergarten, to the fevered and ultimately hopeless smooches he'd exchanged with Melinda Tulley in the back seat of his father's car at the age of nineteen, try as he might to add sight to the magic blend of senses—taste and touch and sound and smell—he couldn't do it. He closed his eyes.

Why? Because kissing was intense. It was *important*. A heck of a lot more important than you'd think, judging by the careless way some people engaged in the activity. He had loved Gloria as only a five-year-old could. He had loved Melinda with the idealism of newly minted adulthood before she'd headed for Chicago and college, never to return.

Since then his relationships with women—two pretty

serious ones, over the years—had failed badly. He hadn't done much kissing lately at all. Both those women had been around his own age, with a child from a previous relationship. Both those times, it had been because of the child—not because of the kissing—that they'd split up.

At the age of twenty-three, he'd gone out with Karine, a hair stylist down in Bozeman, for five months before he'd even discovered she was a mom. For five months, she had lied about it, and when he'd finally found out the truth, she'd said she was scared because of things he'd said. Scared he wouldn't want to take on her child.

"Because of things I said?" he'd echoed, shocked.

And it had set him thinking. Yeah, he'd talked to her about Mitch and Mom and Dad. Dad's anger, Mom's sense of failure. Maybe Karine was right. He was reluctant about it. After that he'd tried for three months to build something with her little Jamie. But he had felt so self-conscious about it, and Karine had watched his every move. He couldn't blame her for that. It hadn't worked and they'd split up.

Then, a few years ago, he'd met Judith in the bank in Blue Rock. She was a wildlife photographer from Seattle, just a little older than he was, in town for a couple of months to work on a book.

She hadn't lied. He had known from the beginning that she had a twelve-year-old daughter, Mara, who was on vacation with Judith's ex-husband. And Gray had been so determined to make it work that he'd started to care about Mara just from hearing Judith talk about her.

They'd had such great times together, scouting out places for Judith to photograph. He'd almost asked her to marry him after the first month, but had decided to wait until Mara arrived for the final month of Judith's stay. It seemed fair. The decent thing to do. He didn't want to spring the relationship on a twelve-year-old when it was already a done deal.

Would it have been different if he hadn't made that honorable decision to wait?

Mara hated Montana from the word go. She missed the city, missed her friends. Judith began to speed up the pace of her work. She began to talk about cutting short her stay.

"But what about us?" he'd asked.

Judith's eyes had skated quickly away from the appeal in his. "It—it wouldn't have worked," she'd told him softly, adding without conviction, "even without the issue of where Mara wants to live."

"But we haven't even talked about the problem. Maybe there are other options. You haven't let me try to tackle it. Give me these few weeks working on it to see if—"

"Tackle it? It's not like breaking in a horse, Gray! Good grief!"

Maybe he should have pushed harder. But he hadn't. Instead, he'd flinched at her comparison and wondered if she was right. He was approaching the whole situation the wrong way. Hell, if his father hadn't been able to win Mitch over and build a relationship with him when they'd lived beneath the same roof for almost fifteen years, what on earth made him think he could do it? Do it *at all*, let alone in a single month?

From that point on, he'd sworn off women with kids. Not just because of Karine. Not just because of Judith. It was around this time that Mitch had trampled on Louise's loving heart yet again, using her, deceiving her, discounting her love. Yet again, Frank had yelled over the phone at his stepson to get out of their lives, if he cared so little about the way he hurt her. This time, Mitch had taken Frank at his word. Hadn't even shown up at his stepfather's funeral, despite Louise's pleading.

Now at last Grayson James McCall was kissing someone else. A woman whom he'd first known as Cinderella, with a smile that would make any man feel like a prince. A woman who was just as hopelessly wrong for him as those other women had been. A woman who, if he ever made the mistake of getting serious about her, would force him into the role that he felt so uncomfortable about, the role his own loving, honorable and impressively capable father had failed at so badly and had disliked so much. A woman with a four-year old child.

Eyes closed or open, he knew he shouldn't be kissing her. Problem was, he couldn't seem to stop.

And yes…yes…kissing—or kissing Jill Brown, anyway—was *definitely* important. How could anything that felt this good not be important? Important enough to make him forget, for a few glorious moments, how wrong it was.

He could feel the heat radiating from her body. Swaying a little closer, he could feel her breasts, soft and giving and deliciously real, against his chest. He'd been wanting to touch them, explore them, *taste* them, for days. He'd imagined over and over how it would feel if he had them spilling into his hands. How their tight, tender peaks would feel against his mouth, so warm and responsive. How she would shudder with need and gasp out his name.

He felt her teeter a little. She was stretched up on her toes to reach his mouth, which had to be hard work for her. Maybe he should help her out a little. His fingers loosened themselves from hers, and his arms closed tightly around her back before he gave himself the chance to work out whether this was an act of kindness, or one of pure, selfish need.

Hell, he *wanted* this woman! Desire surged in him without regard for anything his rational mind could tell him, without regard for the way his wounded heart wanted to harden itself with an armor of rejection.

Now he could feel the bump of her hips as well as the press of her breasts. He could feel the rub of her thighs, the neat shape of her back, the sweet fullness of her mouth and the soft tickle of her dark hair.

The snug-fitting T-shirt began to tease at his imagination. Her body felt great through the fabric, but how much better would it feel with nothing getting in the way? It was a short little garment, showing an inviting half-inch gap between its hem and the waistband of her jeans. He had no trouble sliding his fingers beneath it, then trailing them over the soft skin at her waist and bringing them slowly higher until he reached her breasts.

Lace.

Her bra was made of lace. Which explained the hint of texture he'd noticed every time his eyes had drifted to that general area this morning. And his eyes had drifted there far too frequently, he now realized. He cupped his palms around her fullness, grazed the throbbing peaks of her nipples with his fingertips, felt her shiver with need, then slid his hands back against her sides once more.

Her breasts were great. He could spend hours exploring them. But even more urgently, he wanted to *hold* her. He wanted to gather her close to him and keep her there. He wanted to invade her mouth so relentlessly that neither of them could speak or think.

"Moo-oo…"

Okay, this was another problem about kissing with your eyes closed. All your other senses became that much sharper, including your hearing.

"Moo-oo…"

That was one of his gag-danged, pasture-hopping, far too frisky cows bawling in the background, and he couldn't ignore it any longer. He should be grateful to the beasts for acting as chaperones, for bringing him back to earth.

He *should* be grateful, and he was.

"Jill," he rasped, his throat tight with strain, "we have to go after those animals."

"I know. I'm sorry to…to delay you."

He opened his eyes. She was staring down, breath heaving in and out in a way that did interesting things to her contours and achy things to his groin. Her long black lashes masked the greenness of her eyes. Their unique color was like jade beneath running water.

"Hell, was it your fault?" he said bluntly.

"No, I guess not."

She looked up, and they stared at each other.

She crossed one forearm over the other and curled her fingers around her upper arms. It was getting chilly here in the shade, now that they'd stopped playing hide-and-go-seek with those crazy cows. Was that why she had goose bumps all over her?

No. It wasn't.

They both knew it. They weren't touching anymore, but that didn't mean the pull and the need had gone away. It hadn't. It was stronger than ever. But he was angry at it and fighting it now, with everything he had.

"Let's go get the cattle," he growled harshly. "We've spent long enough on this already."

Jill heard the words with a chill of reluctant agreement. Two seconds would have been "long enough" for that kiss. Ten, maybe fifteen minutes was... stretching it, to say the least.

Neither of them needed this. She had come here for one reason—to get a divorce. Sam's illness was the only reason why she was still here. Doctor's orders. The chemistry was irrelevant, inconvenient and dangerous. And if it made Grayson angry, as it clearly did, then that *shouldn't* feel like a slap in the face. So why were both her cheeks stinging?

"Oh, crud, there's three more of 'em," Gray said, as they approached the thick belt of trees to which the cattle had fled. "Well, I guess that first lot did us a favor, coming in this direction, then, or we wouldn't have spotted them."

"They look a little quieter now," Jill suggested. She could sense the way Gray's muscles were knotted as he moved beside her, like a fighter prepared for a tough round. He still looked grim.

"Like kids," he said, staring them down. "Tired and hungry."

The russet-brown beasts were grazing contentedly, with a sort of, "What, me? Uncooperative?" attitude.

"With any luck we can just walk them back up this trail, here," Gray said. "There's good grazing all the way. That open patch in the sunshine just when they get back on our land should draw them."

"You're not trying to tell me this is going to be easy?" she tried to joke.

With her lips still swollen from Gray's kiss, she felt disoriented and unsettled, her insides churning. They walked side by side in the wake of the cattle, who'd belatedly decided to cooperate, and the silence between them felt too thick. She needed conversation to distract her from the masculine rhythm of his walk and from her sense of his body warmth so close to her. It was a pity that she couldn't think of a single safe thing to say.

Gray was the one to speak first. "That's not going to happen again."

"No…"

"I'm sorry." It came out as rough as sandpaper on splintery wood, betraying his frustration. "It was my fault as much as yours. Don't think I'm suggesting anything else. But it's…where it was starting to go…is impossible."

"I know," she agreed.

"You're hoping to make a life with someone else, and I'm not interested in a woman who comes with—"

He broke off, practically biting the end of the sentence in half, and what he'd been about to say seemed so obvious to Jill that she said it for him.

"With a child. That's what you were going to say, isn't it? Whatever you think you might grow to feel about me, if you let yourself, you'd never want Sam."

"Don't get me wrong, he's a great kid—"

"I'm not going to take the time to 'get' anything, Grayson." Her scalp was tight with anger. "You're saying it as if I'm trying to get a free ride with a man for myself and my child. I told you I had no plans to ask you for a settlement. That was Alan's idea. I'm not going to apologize for it, and I'm not looking for a free ride from him, either, in case you're wondering. We'll be partners, we'll both work hard, and we'll both put our kids first."

"Jill—"

"But you need to rethink a few things. A lot of women come with 'baggage' these days. A lot of men, too, for that matter. And if you can make a non-negotiable decision that women with baggage aren't worth a second look, then you're a shallower person than I thought you were."

"Maybe that's true," he said. "Did you stop to think that's why I might have made a decision like that? Because I know myself? And I know I couldn't do it?"

"How could you know something like that? Have you tried?"

"Twice. And so did my dad. He tried for years. And if a man like Dad couldn't make it work…"

"…Then neither can you. You're comparing yourself with him on this issue just the way you compare yourself with him on the issue of the ranch. Why?''

She was still angry. But the reason had started to change.

''Because he was a good man. A great man. He was clever, he was hardworking, and he loved Mom as if the stars shone out of her smile. He was the man I want to be.''

''And what makes you think you're not? What makes you so sure you're not just as great, Gray?'' she demanded.

''Because I'm not doing it, okay?'' His voice shuddered with feeling and his fists were clenched. ''The ranch is failing, and we're this close to having to sell! *This close, Jill!*'' He raised one hand and pressed his thumb and middle finger together. ''Not just to selling Thurrell Creek but Flaming Hills as well. *That's* how I know I'm not the man Dad was.''

He didn't want to talk about it anymore. That was obvious. He had quickened his pace, and his footfalls were heavy on the rough terrain. But she kept pace with him and they crossed the last section of broken fence-line and back onto McCall land together, with the cows scattering ahead of them, lured by the sun-drenched grass.

Jill's anger had shifted into a different feeling. Something more painful. Something harder to understand. She didn't bother to try, just spoke from the heart.

''You have to let me help for as long as we're here,'' she said, meaning it. ''I know it's not much, but let me do what I can. Every little thing makes a difference, doesn't it? Every piece of fence we fix, every bale of winter feed we store.''

"I appreciate the offer, Jill, but—"

"But! I don't want to hear that word. Don't be so stubborn. And don't deny me the chance to do what's right.''

"Why is it right?" he argued. "You didn't want to get stuck on my ranch. You didn't want Sam to get sick.''

"It's right because we're married, Gray.''

"According to some piece of paper.''

"Okay, I know it doesn't mean for either of us what it usually means for people, but it means something. Let me make it mean a little more, while I have the chance, so that our divorce doesn't negate…what we had.''

"What did we have, Jill?''

Magic. For a few hours, we had magic. You know we did.

The same magic we discovered again today, when we kissed….

Of course she didn't say any of it aloud. Once again, there was a harshness to his voice that rattled her. He didn't need to sound that way. But maybe it was his way of reacting to those explosive minutes in each other's arms. Their kiss had colored things differently for him, just as it had colored things differently for her. But it seemed as if their reactions had gone off in opposite directions.

He wanted to deny everything. Understanding a little more about what drove him, growing to respect even more deeply the man he was, she wanted to hold on, at least, to a memory.

"We had an alliance," she said, struggling to express it right. "We were *friends* that night in Las Vegas. We talked to each other, the way we've talked to each other even more this week. About the ranch. About our dads. It's only on paper, it's only temporary, but I'm your *wife,* Gray, and I'm not going to run out on you without doing everything I can. Even if it's only for the sake of your mother, who's been so good to me."

At this precise moment, they stepped through a gap in the bushes that lined the creek and came face to face with Louise. She was rigid, wide-eyed, open-mouthed and silent. Neither Jill nor Gray were in the slightest doubt that she'd heard everything Jill said.

Including, most particularly, the word "wife."

How could she help it?

I was practically yelling, Jill realized.

Out of the corner of her eye, she glimpsed Grandpa Pete paddling barefoot in the creek with Sam, some distance upstream. They, at least, were out of earshot, thank goodness.

Gray groaned as he registered the expression on his mother's face. He knew she'd heard, too. "It's not important, Mom, okay?"

"Not *important?*"

"It's not what you think."

"You and Jill are *married!* She's your wife!"

"Not really."

"She just said so, Gray!"

"Well, yes, technically—" Jill began.

"Fact is, we are apparently married, on paper," Gray cut in. He sounded like a lawyer, but that tone soon dropped as he continued. "Mom, don't look at us like that! There was this stunt in Las Vegas. That Cinderella Marriage Marathon competition. You remember, we watched it a couple of times on TV?"

"You were a *part* of that?"

"I outbid a couple of sleazy guys. Didn't know what it was about. Didn't think it was a real wedding. Found out afterward that it was. Jill couldn't get hold of me to arrange the divorce. Remember when we couldn't get the new phone line run to the old house, after we rented the new place out? That's why she came here. To see about the divorce."

"I knew it! I've wanted to ask you about it for days. I knew there was something going on. That you two were more to each—"

"There's nothing going *on,* Mom!"

"According to your definition."

"According to *anyone's* definition! We're getting the divorce as soon as we can. We're totally agreed on that."

"Right…" There was a light of lingering suspicion in Louise's eyes, which would have burst into flames if she'd witnessed their kiss.

Gray ignored it.

"We're only fighting," he said, "because Jill has some idea that she owes it to me—to us—to work her backside off while she's here. Which is sweet of her."

"It isn't sweet. I'm never sweet!" Jill's eyes flashed. "But I've been brought up to do what's right, pay my debts, and I'm going to pay this one."

"She doesn't have to."

"I'm right, aren't I?"

They were both appealing to Louise now, standing side by side in front of her, demanding her judgment like two children yelling, "She started it!" "No, he started it!"

Louise gave a helpless, half-hysterical laugh. "Do you two have *any* idea how crazy this is? And how you sound?"

Gray and Jill exchanged sheepish glances, in which sparks of anger and awareness still flared.

"Yeah, like kids," Gray muttered.

"This has nothing to do with me," Louise went on. Her voice was brisk. "Jill, I've never put so much as a dish towel in a guest's hand before, if they weren't begging me for one, but I respect your sense of duty. If you want to get involved in the work of the ranch while you're here, please do. But please don't think that I feel you're in our debt, whether you're Gray's wife 'technically' or 'temporarily' or whatever in the heck other possibilities you both seem to feel there are!"

"Thanks."

Jill knew that her cheeks were glowing. All three of them were silent for a minute, in an uneasy truce.

"Can I just ask you one question? Why do you want a divorce so urgently?" Louise flashed the question at her just as the tension began to drain away. It came rushing back in an instant.

"I want to be free to marry someone else." It sounded too blunt and businesslike and hardheaded.

Which of course it was. She *wanted* that! Jill reminded herself.

Louise nodded slowly. Gray scowled at the sky. Jill swallowed around a painful throat. And this time the silence between them didn't break.

Chapter Seven

"Louise, the doctor thinks I should give it another week or so," Jill reluctantly told the older woman three days later, as they cleared away the breakfast things. Gray must have gone out extra early this morning, because Jill hadn't seen him.

Sam had had a fever and a runny nose yesterday evening, and she had panicked and gotten Gray to drive her into town once more. Just a cold, not a complication from his chicken pox, Dr. Blankenship said, soothing her fears. She'd checked his ears and found that both of them were red, suggesting an ear infection. It made sense. Sam had complained that his ears and throat hurt. The doctor wrote out a prescription for some antibiotics.

Nothing to get overly concerned about, she said. But it confirmed her initial opinion that Sam needed to be thoroughly well again before they set out for home.

"Have you told Gray about your plans?" Louise asked, rattling the dishes in the sink.

"Not yet." She could easily have done so on the way home from the doctor last night, but she hadn't.

Her admission, tinged once again with unconscious reluctance, was rewarded by one of those shrewd, silent, slightly alarmed—and very alarm*ing*—looks from Louise that Jill was starting to recognize. And dread. How did Louise get that uncanny ability to act as if life was a movie that she had already seen twice before?

"I'll tell him, if you like," Louise offered.

"Thanks. We'll definitely be here until next Monday. It's fine if you tell him. That way he can—" She stopped.

"Plan?" Louise suggested.

"Plan. Yes."

They put in some hard work over the next few days. Gray and Jill were first up each morning, but the other adults soon followed. For once in her life, Jill could have handled sleeping in. She envied Sam, still warm and fast asleep in his little bed, as she tiptoed around him in the near darkness, getting dressed.

Sam had taken the news that they might be staying a few extra days in his stride, with a child's easy acceptance.

"Till my cold's better? And my ear?" He snuffled and coughed.

"That's right."

"Are we having a vacation?" he asked.

"You are, honey. The doctor thinks you need one. But Mommy's going to try and help out."

Fortunately, the sort of clothes she'd packed for sitting on a train, arranging a divorce and seeing Chicago in the fall worked okay for getting down and dirty on a ranch as well. The Indian summer mildness was replaced once more by a frosty fall chill, and once, briefly, there was snow. She had to borrow a couple of warmer garments from Louise.

And then she worked. Worked and cared for Sam and spent hours of every day with Gray. They cleaned grain bins and stored winter salt, repaired the bale retriever, changed the oil in the truck... She lost count of the different ways she spent each day.

Gray told her a lot about the life of the ranch as they worked. Maybe it was the only safe subject he could think of. She got a review lesson on Sam's lecture about the diseases of cattle, and this time some of it stuck. She heard about the fifteen different kinds of noxious weeds that Gray was required, by Montana state law, to keep in check. She learned that not all sections of this ranch could grow their own grass without help. There wasn't enough rain. In the summer months, the McCalls needed to irrigate by using portable dams, which were hard work to fix in place.

She started to understand the seasonal rhythm of the work, heard in Gray's voice the things he loved about his life, and the things he feared. Range fires, like the terrible ones last summer. Locust plagues. Late storms. Bad cattle prices.

Did the rewards really compensate? she asked him on Thursday evening as they walked back to the house together. With all the hardships, were the rewards really enough?

He shrugged at the question. It was a shrug she recognized now. It said, "Don't make me try to put this into words." But then he put it into words anyhow, with a rusty, clunky sort of explanation that arrowed its way straight into her heart.

"Ranching is in my blood. Times I think it'd be easier if I hated it, like my brother Mitchell did, and could give it up. He spent years trying to convince Dad to sell, and trying to funnel the profits of the place into his own pocket. But I always loved it. Even the worst days, you know you've really *done* something. And the best days, ah, the best days! When spring comes and the cattle are healthy and the sky is blue. And I'm up there on Highboy with the sun on my back and a good breakfast in my stomach. You feel like you're going to burst with it."

Jill nodded. "Mm-hm." Couldn't say anything more.

It was almost dark. The chill was biting, and Jill had blisters on her hands that throbbed. But she knew that Louise and Sam and Pete would already be inside, and that Louise would have the evening meal hotted up and ready to put on the table.

She could see shadows moving behind the curtains that glowed yellow from the lamps lit here and there. It wasn't the same kind of "best day" that Gray had just described, but it felt good all the same. Magically, dangerously, deceptively good.

She had a bursting feeling of her own and she was fighting it all the way. She didn't want to feel this way about the slow, liquid darkness in his voice or about the thought and care that pooled in his black eyes, about the work-hardened calluses on his hands or the deep tan on the back of his neck.

She'd told herself this so many times—that she could never fall seriously for a man who didn't want her child. That her best possible future lay with Alan. The problem was that when Sam wasn't around, all the tension between herself and Gray disappeared and the magic came flooding back.

"That's all it is," she reminded herself. "*Black* magic. Betrayal and deception, and all coming from inside *me*. Why can't I make it disappear?"

They reached the steps that led up to the back porch and Gray stood back to let her go first. She felt the aura of his warmth and strength as she passed him, gritted her teeth and counted the days.

Two more.

Today's Saturday. We're leaving on Monday.

Two more days. Jill had called Ron Thurrell and arranged to pick up a one-way car rental at his garage. She would return the car in Trilby. Gray had said he would drive Jill and Sam into Blue Rock on Monday morning.

Sam's course of antibiotics was nearly finished, and it had kept in check any further secondary infections. Dr. Blankenship had asked a series of searching questions at their appointment yesterday and had given her official approval for Sam to travel.

"All the same, you should get off the train in Chicago and take that vacation with your boyfriend," she had decreed.

"He's still not sure that he can make it."

"*Make* him make it. Just get off the train, check into an expensive hotel, then call him and tell him you need him to come and take care of the bill."

Jill had just laughed at this. She didn't want to admit to Dr. Blankenship that Alan wouldn't respond to that kind of impulsive blackmail. He believed in both of them taking their budget seriously and wasn't looking to rescue her from some plight of her own making.

And he was right. Getting rescued could bring on more problems than it solved.

Like the problem of having to deal with her over-the-top reaction to how Grayson McCall looked in his best jeans.

Two more days...

Jill and Sam had just arrived with the McCalls and Grandpa Pete at the big evening cookout, which a nearby ranching family put on each year at this time. There were dozens of impressions to absorb about the Sheehans' ranch. Instead, all she could think about was a particular piece of cut and stitched denim.

Okay, so they were different jeans. Not the ones he'd thrown in the laundry hamper an hour ago, before his shower, covered from waist to ankle in stains Jill wouldn't have been able to recognize two weeks ago. But still, they were only jeans. Blue. Stitched. Riveted. Pocketed. New enough to be unfaded. Old enough to—

Jill took a steadying breath and revised her opinion. It wasn't the jeans. It was the body inside the jeans. Jeans which were old enough to give softly in all the places that counted. Covering his thighs. Across his tight backside.

His jeans were a classic fit, the kind that didn't narrow at the waist, and this drew her attention to the fact that there was not one quarter inch of fat there, beneath the clean white Western shirt he wore. His body was all lean muscle, worked and contoured from all the hours of leaning and twisting, lifting and hauling that he did every day. Better than any number of trips to a city gym. Jill knew. She'd been watching how he worked for nearly two weeks, now.

At five in the evening, the big shed on the Sheehans' family ranch was already packed and noisy, with a near-even mix of men and women, and handfuls of excited kids thrown in as well. Sam clung close to her and held her hand, a little overwhelmed by the event. His head was still a little clogged up but that was all. Even his spots had begun to fade.

Grandpa Pete hadn't made it into the shed yet. He'd been corralled by a cluster of older men taking it easy and warming their hands around the huge, homemade cookout brazier out front. The salty smell of cooking meat was strong enough to follow Gray, Jill and Sam all the way inside.

The country music band was almost ready to play. They were up on the makeshift stage, testing their instruments with a painful lack of harmony. Sam grinned at the antics of two pint-size cowboys just a little older than himself. He wasn't yet bold enough to go and join them, but it wouldn't be long before he did.

"Let's get something to eat and drink," Gray said.

He edged Jill, Sam and himself closer to the tables where everything was laid out. The first piled platters of barbecue meat had just been brought inside, the salads and breads were waiting, and people were interested. It was getting more and more crowded near the tables, until Jill and Gray were pressed up hard against each other, and all the familiar sensations generated by her touch and her heat flowed over him.

When they reached the food, Gray stood back a little to watch, while Jill consulted with Sam about what he wanted to eat. She was such a great mom. She didn't order or cajole, just discussed the issue in a sensible way.

"A hot dog is fine, Sam."

"Chips?"

"Chips, too." She reached for two plates and a pair of serving tongs, and began to pile things on, juggling it all with expertise. "Now, are you going to come back for seconds, or have it all on one plate, honey?"

"All on one plate."

"Then let's take some watermelon, too, because you haven't had any fruit today, and this looks so juicy and sweet."

"Do I get Coke?"

"Sure, honey, and there's fruit punch with ice in it, too, if you want some of that. You're going to get thirsty if you run around with the other kids."

She's going to have to brush her arm past my shoulder again, to give Sam his food, Gray realized. He was waiting for it, he knew. He wanted it.

But before Jill could hand Sam his plate, Gray felt the rougher contact of a far less welcome body than hers. Ron Thurrell had barged in behind them, eager to eat. From the smell of his breath, Gray could tell that he'd already been drinking for quite a while.

The alcohol had loosened his tongue. "Grayson

McCall, I do declare! Shouldn't you be at ho-ome on your two ranches, with your noge...your nose to the grindstone?''

He held his face just inches from Gray's. The crowd made it impossible to pull away. No one was attempting to give them any space. Maybe people wanted to hear this. It was well known that the McCalls and the Thurrells didn't have much time for each other.

Thurrell hadn't seen Sam, and his beer belly squashed against the back of Sam's head.

"Watch the little boy!" Gray told him sharply.

But the man hadn't even heard. He was rambling and his words were slurred. "You wait. You w-wait, McCall! You're going to shell to me. I'm gonna make you sh—sell to me. Can't expand your holding with no capital. Your dad was smart. He knew that, and I know it. You wait, McCall!''

He laughed, then swung around and elbowed his way impatiently to the table. Something hard in his hip pocket whipped against Sam's ear, and the little boy flinched back, pressed his hand to the side of his head and looked as though he might cry.

Jill gave a sound of dismay, but she was still holding the two filled plates at shoulder height, and couldn't reach the table to put them down. Gray didn't hesitate. He forgot about Thurrell's drunken ravings, just bent down to Sam.

"You okay?"

"He hurt my ear."

"He was clumsy, wasn't he?" Gray squeezed Sam's shoulders in a rough hug. "He didn't notice. Not your fault, okay? Getting better now?"

"Yup. It's fine now."

"Good kid!"

"Thanks, Gray," Jill said.

She sent Sam to sit on one of the chairs by the far wall, then waited beyond the thickest part of the crowd while Gray filled a plate for himself. His mother and grandfather were still caught up in groups of friends, catching up on the news. There were people here that Gray could have spent time with, too, but somehow, beyond a few nods and casual greetings, that didn't happen.

Instead, he sat and ate with Jill and Sam, then got some fruit punch for Jill and a second beer for himself, and watched Sam make friends with the other kids.

It shouldn't have been a good place to talk. The band was playing, people were yelling and laughing and dancing. The noise level was high. Seated side by side against the shed's metal wall, he and Jill had to lean close to hear what the other was saying.

Maybe that was how it happened. They were leaning close. And somehow that translated into *feeling* close. Their thoughts. Their mood. The things they wanted to say. Afterward, he couldn't have tracked the way the subject of their conversation flowed and changed. All he knew was that suddenly they were talking about love, and he'd forgotten about Ron Thurrell, about Mom, about Grandpa, about everyone.

"Do you believe in it, Gray?" Jill sounded helpless, as if she were looking for answers. It surprised him, because until now he'd been pretty convinced she had more answers than he did. "Do you know what it is?"

Well, hell, he'd never been able to resist this woman

when she needed something from him, had he? For a simple, tongue-tied cattleman, he got pretty eloquent, under the influence of those jewel-green eyes looking big and wide into his. Didn't even hear the noise around them anymore.

"Not sure if I know what it is," he said, taking it carefully. "But, yeah, I believe in it, and I know what it requires. I'm sure of that. Love requires greatness in a person."

"Greatness?"

"I think it takes strength and courage to really love someone. I think the ability to truly love is a sign of greatness...just greatness of heart, I guess. The best people I've known in my life have been the ones who really knew...or know...how to love."

"Don't you think that you have greatness of heart, Gray?"

She had her legs crossed and her arms wrapped around her knees. One protectively rounded shoulder brushed his upper arm, and he felt every single hair stand on end beneath his shirt.

"I don't know," he answered her, hearing the catch in his own voice. "I'm hoping some day I'll find out. I'd like to have what Mom and Dad built between them."

"So you must think I'm pretty ordinary, because I'm planning to marry without that?" Her green eyes were clouded beneath a tight frown.

He had to think for a little before he could answer this one right.

"I guess I don't think you really will marry without

love, when it comes to the point. You have the wrong idea about what love is, is all."

"You mean you think I won't marry Alan?"

"No, I mean that you'll love Alan. It'll grow on you. On both of you. Slowly, like moss growing on a tree. The only reason you're even thinking about marrying him is because you have an intuition that it's going to happen. I think for most people, it's intuition at first. Love doesn't click on like a light bulb. The intuition clicks on, and the love—the real, slow-growing love— comes later."

"Maybe. Or maybe love isn't as important as respect and teamwork and shared priorities," she said, lifting her chin and squaring her small, determined jaw.

"Like your kids?"

"Sam comes first." Her chin went even higher.

He sensed it was a phrase she'd repeated to herself countless times. And he didn't agree with it! He'd been observing their relationship, even if reluctantly, and he didn't agree with what she said.

"Doesn't Sam's happiness depend on yours? Could he be happy if you were miserable? Could you give him what he needed if you were miserable?"

"If Sam is happy, I won't be miserable," she said, parrot-like. Something else she'd told herself many times before. She was leaning back against the shed's metal side now, her arms folded defensively beneath her breasts. "If Sam's happy, I'll be happy."

"You're wrong," he told her quietly. "It won't be like that. It never is. It has to go both ways. You have to find something that works for both of you."

Seeing the stubborn shape of her mouth and the high

color in her cheeks, he didn't say anything more. He wondered if he'd said too much already. Why put doubts into her mind? She had seemed so clear and confident about her plans, about Alan, and he had nothing to offer in their place.

Or did he? For just a moment, he caught a breathtaking glimpse of something magical, something akin to what his parents had had, despite the problems between Dad and Mitch.

Then the doubt came flooding back in, and he muttered aloud, "I can see it. Doesn't mean I can achieve it. That's what's so *hard....*"

"Sorry, Gray?" She looked puzzled for a few seconds, then her brow cleared. "Oh, wait, I know. You're talking about the ranch. You're talking about your father, and the ranch."

He acknowledged the truth of it with a short nod. Probably he was. Everything came back to his dad and the ranch at the moment. Everything came back to his dad, whose sudden loss was still tearing at his heart.

"Is that wrong?" he asked. "To measure myself against the best man I've ever known?"

Jill heard the intense, emotional question and understood exactly what it said about the kind of man Gray was. She rebelled. "You've got to stop doing this, Gray!"

"Doing what?"

"Measuring yourself that way."

Instinctively, she pivoted toward him and felt her knee press into his thigh. He sat up a little straighter, his black eyes fixed on her face. In the region of their thighs, denim pressed against denim, and she didn't want to cut the contact. She had to clasp her hands together in her lap to keep from putting one of them on his body. On his thigh or his arm, or against his jaw.

"Everyone's different," she went on, her voice getting husky. "Their situations are different, and their strengths are different. I can't believe he was a better man than you are. Maybe he was wrong about the purchase of the Thurrell Creek ranch. Have you thought about that? You know, everybody runs their own race in this life, Gray. Stop looking sideways at the race your dad ran, and just start running your own."

Something warm and loud and alive catapulted out of the crowd in her direction at this moment and hurled itself at her lap. It was her son.

"Mommy, can we go explore? The kids say there are kittens and eggs to collect. I want to collect eggs," he gabbled in a breathless voice. His dark hair stood up wildly all over his head and displayed several stalks of straw. He dragged a tissue from his pocket and snuffled into it.

Jill immediately frowned. "Maybe you should take a break," she said. "You've tired yourself out."

"I don't want to go home yet."

"I didn't say go home. Okay, we'll explore, but promise you won't go nuts, Sam. Let's take it quietly."

"Okay, real quietly, I promise. Let's go!"

"I'm coming."

Instinctively, she looked back at Gray, but he shook his head. "Going to talk to some people," he said, the familiar roughness back in his voice.

She let it go, wondering what he'd thought of her

little lecture. She had meant it, and she'd meant it for the best. He wasn't the kind of man to reject a woman's words out of hand, but maybe she'd overstepped the bounds. They'd each given the other something to think about, at any rate. What he'd said to her kept echoing in her head as she and Sam found the kittens and hunted for eggs around the poultry yard.

Love starts with intuition and grows slowly.

That didn't reflect her own experience. She had fallen head over heels for Sam's father, Curtis. Head over heels into what, though? A frenzy of teenage need and wanting, and the sense of having won a glittering prize coveted by a dozen other girls. She'd met Curtis through his younger sister, who skated at the ice rink in Philly and trained with Jill's coach. And Jill had felt a secret triumph that, out of all the other rink girls, she was the one he'd chosen. She hadn't understood just how short-lived his interest would be.

Was that love? No.

She hadn't seen it at the time, but she could see it now.

And Alan?

Love grows slowly, like moss on a tree, Gray had said. *It's intuition at first.*

What was her starting point with Alan? She didn't have a name for it, but the word that Gray had used didn't fit.

And if love could grow slowly over the years, so could other things, couldn't they? Things like disillusion, rejection, coldness and despair....

"I found an egg! Mommy, I found one!"

"That's great, Sam."

Using his excitement as the excuse for a hug, she held him as if she might never let him go, the doubts still whirling in her mind. Her child seemed like the only fixed point in her universe, right now.

Her child, and some heartfelt words from Grayson McCall. She felt as if she could have sat beside him in that noisy, crowded shed all night as they each tried to talk out...tried to make sense of...the tangle of feelings that filled their hearts.

"There's no need for you and Gray to leave, Jill," Louise said brightly, an hour later.

Sam was so tired—very contentedly tired, with four eggs nestled safely in an egg carton to take back to the McCalls—that he had fallen asleep on the back seat of Louise's station wagon.

Louise had insisted on them bringing both the pick-up and the station wagon this evening, in case some of their little party of five were ready to head for home before others. It seemed to be working out exactly that way.

"The dancing has started, and they're going to serve ice cream, soon," she went on. "Sam's already asleep, and he knows me well enough now that I can carry him up to his bed at home without him getting disoriented. So stay. You've both earned it!"

Without waiting for an answer, she bundled up her jacket like a pillow and tucked it under Sam's head.

Grandpa Pete told his daughter a little tetchily, "Should have saved your jacket to put on top of him, not underneath him."

"There's a blanket in the truck, Dad," she soothed him patiently. "I'll get that."

Gray and Jill looked at each other. Pete was climbing into the front of the station wagon. Louise would drive, and Sam was stretched the whole way across the back seat, with the center seat belt fastened around his waist.

"Looks like it's a done deal," Gray said. "Could you handle some ice cream?"

"That would be nice," Jill answered.

She wondered what else he was offering, and what else she had promised with her reply.

Louise and Pete drove off a minute or two later, with Pete still worrying out loud about how they were going to get Sam out of the station wagon, up the stairs, into his pajamas and into bed without disturbing him. Jill had no doubt that Louise would manage very well. The grandmotherly woman had a satisfied expression on her face and was taking no notice of Pete's anxiety at all.

Jill was less convinced about her own ability to manage the rest of the evening here with Gray. Louise surely hadn't engineered this deliberately, had she? Why do a thing like that? She couldn't possibly want anything deeper to grow between her son and some single mother city girl who'd blown in from Philly, in need of a quick divorce.

Louise was a practical woman. She would see the obstacles as clearly as Gray and Jill did, themselves. Yet the weird conviction remained. Louise had engineered this, as smooth as silk. She wanted the two of them to be alone together in the middle of this crowded party.

Alone, eating ice cream and dancing.

Chapter Eight

Gray hadn't danced with a woman this way in a long time.

He should have known Jill would dance well. He'd seen her dance across the ice as if her feet were wearing wings instead of stiff boots and metal blades. The fact that she danced well came as no surprise. It was the fact that she could get *him* to dance well that astonished him.

A set of square dances came first. He and Jill got pulled into a group with three couples whom he knew only slightly. All of them had done it before. Jill hadn't, she said. But she had music in her blood and she was used to following instructions about how to move her body. It took her a few minutes to understand some of the basic terms, though Gray himself wasn't any help in teaching her.

"Sashay left? Well, that's when you—" he began, then tailed off.

"Copy me, honey," one of the other women, named Doris, said to Jill. "Henry? We'll show her this time around."

Soon Jill's feet were flying and she was laughing. Their arms linked and slid apart. Gray had his arm around her waist, then around Doris Kring's. That felt completely wrong. Back with Jill again, his heart soared. Her hips rocked and her breasts bounced just the right amount. She smiled at him, flirted with him in the way she tossed glances at him over her shoulder, and in the way she cozied up to another partner, then swung back into Gray's arms again.

Flirting was permissible in dancing. Flirting and dancing were fun, and Gray found himself thinking hazily and happily that in future he'd do this more often, this dancing stuff, as long as Jill was his partner.

Which she wouldn't be, he realized.

His heart dropped into his boots just as his boots hit the floor, at the end of the music. The dance was over. So was his time with Jill. She and Sam were heading home on Monday.

Suddenly, square dancing was no longer enough for him. He wanted more. He wanted to make the very most of this while he still could. Someone was on his side, apparently. The band's dance caller announced that he was now the band's singer, and there was going to be a change of mood.

Yep, Elvis was definitely a change of mood. The guy launched into a wobbly and very over-done medley of the King's best-known love songs, starting with "Love Me Tender," and Gray had Jill wrapped tight in his arms before he'd even paused for breath.

Let alone for thought.

She didn't look like she was planning an escape, either. Instead, she nestled into him, laid her head on his shoulder and pressed her hands flat against the back pockets of his jeans. She pulled him even closer.

Oh, lord! She'd be able to feel just what this was doing to him…!

But apparently she didn't mind.

"Mmm…"

He felt her sigh against his neck, and it made every hair on his body prickle and sit up straight. Her hands slid down just a little, to the undefined creases at the tops of his thighs.

"Cowboys look so good in jeans," she murmured.

"So do cowgirls," he managed to answer.

"I'm not a cowgirl."

"No, but you look *so* good in jeans that I can't think straight. I don't know what you are anymore, Jill, or who you are. All I know is that I want you here. In my arms. Like this."

All night.

The words hung in the air, but he didn't say them. Didn't dare. They would be legally married for a few months longer, and he wanted her more than he'd ever wanted any woman. But spending the night with her, when she was leaving in two days, wasn't like stealing a farewell kiss.

Spending the night with her would be a beginning, not an ending, and the thing he needed to find right now was a way of ending this.

Couldn't.

Can't.

End this? I don't want to end this.

His body told him that the very idea, the very word, was insane.

End it? No! Embrace it. Give in to it. Go with it. Surrender.

Surrender seemed like such a sweet, sweet word, tonight.

A shuddering sigh racked his body and he turned his head, captured her mouth and kissed her dizzy and breathless and trembling, with his eyes closed, while some guy who didn't look or sound like Elvis went through at least half a dozen more songs.

When he launched into "Jailhouse Rock," Jill was still locked in Gray's arms and he felt like he'd thrown away the key. Her breasts were tight, warm mounds against his chest, and he could feel the way the heat low in her body mingled with his.

It took both of them quite a while to realize that "Jailhouse Rock" wasn't a swoony love song. Several more couples in the big, darkened barn seemed to be having the same trouble. More power to them! Gray understood just how they felt.

"Do you want to go home?" he said to her, thinking of his room and his bed and the darkness, and the fact that they were married—didn't matter how or why it had happened—and maybe it was time they explored what that actually meant. Explored the possibilities it opened up.

Oh, yes, the possibilities...

"Home?" Jill echoed. Her voice sounded fuzzy...and disappointed.

"I mean so we can, uh, talk," he said. They'd had

such a good talk, earlier. He was still thinking about some of the things she'd said. Still, he wasn't really talking about meaningful conversation now, and she knew it. "Just the two of us. I want to—I could do this all night, Jill."

There! He'd said it.

His heart was leaping like a puppy in his chest. He ran his hands down the sides of her jeans, claiming her body, locking his hips against hers, and she didn't move away. She only moved—if this was possible—even closer.

"I want to do this. I want to hold you…" His mouth drank in the taste of her once more and his hands came up to sear her breasts. They were hard at the peaks. "All night."

"Oh, Gray…"

Somehow, they made it to the pickup. Somehow, he drove. They didn't talk. He felt so full of crazy, impetuous words that he didn't dare let his mouth open in case every one of them came spilling out.

She put her cheek on his shoulder and her hand on his thigh, and said his name just once. "Gray…"

There was such a complex mix of need and fear in her tone that he had to take one arm off the wheel, slide it around her shoulders and pull her against his chest. He could hardly stand to take his arm away again when they reached the next bend.

When they got home…

"Mom's left the kitchen light on for us," he said.

He stopped in the middle of the yard, needing the darkness for a little longer. At once she turned into his arms, as if she needed it, too. It was a mild night. Too mild for this time of year. There was a fuzz of cloud thickening over the moon, and he knew instinctively, in the back of his mind, that there would be a storm within a day or two.

They still had cattle to move, winter feed to store. He didn't care. For once in his life, he wasn't thinking about the ranch, wasn't trying to second-guess what Dad would have planned.

"Jill, I want you like crazy." He caressed her fine-boned jaw and lifted her face so he could see into the depths of her eyes. They were huge and soft, just like her mouth. "I don't know how to say it any better than that. And I don't just mean… You *know* I don't just mean…"

"I know. I know, Gray."

She touched the back of his neck and he felt the light friction of her nails. Then her fingers threaded up through his hair and he shuddered and couldn't think about what else they needed to say to cement this. He just wanted to drown in her mouth, to drown in her whole body. Drown in her giving and their shared need.

He had to drag his feet forward with a mighty effort of will, still holding her, or they would never have reached the house, and he wasn't going to drop to the ground and make love to her out in the yard. He didn't plan to stop in the lit-up kitchen, either. They would just go straight up the stairs as quietly as they could, and—

Not possible.

"Mom?" His voice was a croak. "What are you doing, still up?"

He knew it had to be late.

The outer storm door crashed behind him, its hinges screeching. At his side, he felt Jill's warm hand slide from his grasp, then heard her gently close the inner door.

Seated at the kitchen table, Louise looked up from the mug of hot tea she had been staring into and he saw her red-rimmed eyes and puffy nose. She didn't speak.

"What's happened?" The breath and strength went out of him like a burst paper bag and he dropped into the nearest chair. "It's not Grandpa, is it?"

Jill refilled the kettle and put it on the stove. Gray felt her sudden tension as if he was still touching her and understood her need to do something practical with her hands.

Louise tried to smile. "No, it's fine. It's all right. But I had a call from Mitch tonight, that's all..."

Gray's stomach flipped and sank.

To hell with you, big brother! he thought. You call, at last, after two years. It should have made her happy, but no, still it ends like this, with Mom in tears. How come you still have to do this to her? You're thirty-six years old!

"What'd he say?" he growled. "What's he done?"

"Nothing." She gulped. "It's— Just let me tell you, okay? It wasn't strictly accurate to say that he called. His...girlfriend, I guess you'd have to say. She was the one. She called. Told me she'd been trying to convince him to do it for more than six months. Six months! Gray, they have a son."

"A son!"

"He and this girl—she sounded nice, her name's

Lena—have a six and a half month old baby son named Cody, and I didn't even know. If Lena hadn't wanted the baby to meet his grandmother, if she hadn't pushed Mitch about it, how long before he would have told me?''

Her tears freshened. The kettle boiled. Quietly, Jill topped up Louise's tea and poured two more cups.

"How long have you been sitting here?" Gray asked.

She shrugged. "An hour, hour and a half. I knew I wouldn't sleep."

"Congratulations on becoming a grandmother, Louise," Jill said softly, and bent to give her a hug.

"Thanks, honey." Louise gave a watery smile as she returned it. Then she went on, "I mean, it's good news. It is! I'm a Gramma! The baby's healthy and doing fine. Smiling and laughing, putting on weight, getting ready to crawl. He's got brown eyes and curly hair, Lena said. I kind of sensed she's hoping Mitch will marry her. But, you know, when would I ever have found out, if she hadn't called?'' she repeated.

Not for a long time. Neither of them said it, but they both knew. The baby must have been just a week or two old when Gray saw Mitch in Las Vegas in March, but Mitch hadn't said a word.

"You'll want to go see the little guy as soon as you can, I guess," he said. "Lena wanted you to, right? And it would be a chance for you and Mitch to—"

"You know I can't go, Gray," Louise answered. "Not the way things are, right now. I'll…just have to wait and see him when he's older."

Her tone and manner said that she was shrugging it

off, but he saw the way she was gripping her mug so that it shook. Her fingers were so tense and tight that they looked like claws.

"Like when?" he demanded.

"Oh, you know, in a—in a—" She couldn't go on. A year? Two? It would take that long, at least, before things were any easier on this ranch. If they were lucky.

"No!" he told her. The word was practically an explosion. "That's not right. It's going to be a heck of a lot sooner than that, Mom, okay?"

"How?" she demanded. "Just how, Gray?"

"Somehow. I don't care how. We'll just make it possible. Next month, okay? No, I'm not hearing any different!"

He was practically yelling, but Louise took no notice. She was already coming at him with all the reasons why it wasn't possible.

"I'm *not listening* to this!" he repeated. "We'll make it happen."

"I can't go to Las Vegas. We have to be realistic."

"You're going," he said again, savagely this time.

And he didn't know how long they might have gone on stubbornly yelling their impossible positions on the issue if Jill hadn't cut across their increasingly heated words.

"Excuse me, but that's Sam crying. Sounds like he's had a nightmare, and you don't need me here to—"

She left the room without finishing her sentence, and Gray was alone with his mother.

She said, "I was hoping you two would stay outside a little longer so I could get myself together. I didn't

want to spoil your evening. I knew it'd end like this.
I'm sorry, Gray.''

Then she rose from the table, leaving the rest of her
tea untouched, and followed Jill up the stairs. Her exit
was every bit as awkward as Jill's had been.

Left alone, Gray wanted to swear. Seriously considered it. Examined all the possible curse words at his
disposal and rejected every single one of them. What
use was profanity? Prayer would be a lot better, but
even that, in terms of immediate, tangible solutions,
was unlikely to yield a miracle.

He felt helpless and miserable and sick. Gulping the
tea Jill had made, just because it was there, he felt the
bitterness of the tannin in his mouth like a physical
embodiment of his mood.

He knew his mother's stubbornness, her priorities
and her pride. He also knew what was in her heart.
He'd told Jill about his mother's life in snatches over
the past few days, as they worked, in the same way
that Jill had shared details with him about her own
family.

He knew about Jill's difficult, self-absorbed and ma-
nipulative mother, Rose. He knew about her biological
father, who had deserted them more than twenty years
ago and hadn't been heard of since. He knew about her
much-loved stepfather, who'd died several years ago,
and about her sister Suzanne and stepsister Catrina. The
three of them, plus Sam, lived together with an eccentric elderly cousin of Cat's long-deceased mother,
named Pixie, and Gray would have had to be a far less
sensitive man than he was to miss the love in Jill's
voice when she spoke of them.

He wondered if she had read as much between the lines about Louise as Gray himself had read about Jill and the people she loved.

Louise had grown up just near here, on the small ranch that Grandpa Pete and Gramma Alice owned and ran. It wasn't a big enough spread to return a livable profit, and Pete had owned the hardware store in Blue Rock as well.

Blaine Kruger blew into town when Louise Marr was just seventeen. He was a cocky young gun, then aged twenty-five, on the look-out for property to buy on the cheap—places that were being sold off by the bank for nonpayment of mortgage or taxes—which he would then sell for a profit.

He didn't find the pickings quite as rich as he'd hoped, but he made enough to set himself up in Las Vegas, and stayed here long enough that when he left, Louise left with him as his bride. She was eighteen when Mitchell was born, nineteen when her marriage fell apart due to Blaine's repeated infidelity, and twenty when she came back with her little son to Montana. She met Franklin McCall in her dad's hardware store a few months later, and they married when she was twenty-two.

After this, she had played the custody and access thing by the book. Blaine Kruger got to see his son every summer vacation, every second Christmas, and as many times in between as Louise could manage. Gray still didn't know if Blaine had deliberately set about winning Mitch's loyalty for himself, or whether it had been an accidental by-product of their matching

temperaments and the expensive gifts Blaine had show-
ered on him at every visit.

Whatever the reason, it had started early. Gray could
remember, from the time he himself was around five
or six years old, Mitch's regular complaint. ''I hate this
stinking ranch!'' Mitch had left to join his father in Las
Vegas at the age of nineteen, and now he was a very
wealthy man.

Meantime, Gray had never been in the slightest danger of adopting his elder half-brother's opinion. He'd
always loved this place. There had never been so much
as a moment of his life when he'd seen his future lying
anywhere else, and his parents and grandparents all
knew it.

When Gramma Alice died eight years ago, Grandpa
Pete had sold his hardware store and his ranch. He'd
then insisted on razing what they often called ''the old,
new house''—Jill had laughed at that—up on the far
hill, and paying for the construction of ''the new, new
house'' on the same site.

''This is part of Gray's future,'' he'd said, and he
had plowed everything he had into Flaming Hills ever
since.

Gray knew how it hurt Grandpa Pete to see that spa-
cious new place rented out to some Hollywood mil-
lionaire who was hardly ever there, purely to generate
a little cash flow. Meanwhile, this old place, hauled
here from heaven knew where about eighty years
ago—it was surprisingly cozy but not exactly in the
best of shape—wasn't a bunkhouse for single ranch
hands anymore, but had become their family home.

Now, to top everything off, Gray was fighting with

his mother because she knew, and he refused to accept, that she couldn't even spare the time, for the foreseeable future, to visit her new grandson.

How had everything ended up such a mess? And how could he even begin to think of taking Jill to bed tonight, when she was leaving on Monday and his life was like this?

He couldn't. He knew it. Not in a million years.

Tossing the rest of the tea into the sink, he headed up the stairs.

"Was it a nightmare?"

"Mm-hm," Jill whispered.

Sam was still crying into her shoulder when Gray came upstairs. She was pacing the passage outside her bedroom door, and her arms had to be just about pulling from their sockets by now. She'd been doing this for several minutes, but it didn't seem to be helping.

"It must have been a bad one," Gray suggested.

"I think he got overtired tonight," she said. "And he ended up having a lot more soda and cake than his stomach could handle. Do you have a tummy ache, or something, sweetie?"

"And I'm thirsty."

"So your tummy does hurt?" she repeated, to get a clearer answer.

"Yes."

"Let me go get you some water."

"Shall I hold him for a minute?" Gray suggested. He held out his arms, adding, "And maybe we have something he could take for his stomach."

"No! Not medicine!" Sam recoiled in horror.

Gray was holding him, and Jill had let go. Now, all at once, Sam was pushing so hard against Gray's chest that he practically dropped the child, and he was appalled by the look of distrust on Sam's face.

"I want Mommy!" he said urgently. "I don't want you."

He twisted around in Gray's arms and reached for Jill, who had no choice but to take him back again. When he was safely snuggled against her once more, he frowned darkly at Gray, as if he thought he was going to be kidnapped.

"He's just tired," she said.

Louise had said that a dozen times, in Gray's childish hearing, as an apology to Frank for a piece of rudeness from Mitch. The memory echoed inside him painfully. Frank had never been impressed by her reasoning. He had thought she was being soft on her elder son, condoning his unacceptable behavior.

"I'll get him some water," Gray said. "No medicine, okay, Sam?" He kept his voice upbeat, didn't betray what he felt.

A minute later, Sam sipped the water, asked to go to the bathroom, then said his tummy felt better. Gray took the empty water glass back down to the kitchen, while Jill tucked Sam into bed again.

She watched him for a moment, feeling her love for him like something alive and hot inside her. She stroked his face, sang him a very soft song. His eyes drifted shut and she tiptoed out.

"He's asleep," she reported to Gray in the corridor.

"He didn't hear Mom and me...uh...talking, did

he?'' Gray whispered back. ''I was worried that was what woke him up, initially.''

''No, he was overtired, and thirsty, and there were those three slices of cake! Besides, he just has nightmares sometimes. This hasn't been an easy year for him. You know we had that fire in Cousin Pixie's house I told you about, back in July. That unsettled him a lot. I—I worry about it.''

''He's such a great kid, Jill. You don't need to worry that much about him. He's on the right track. I'm sure of it.''

''Thanks. I appreciate your saying that.''

They were both reaching out to each other, mending fences, but Jill sensed it wasn't enough. Not enough to bring back what they'd had, half an hour earlier. The promise of a night together, and the beginnings of something more.

''I'm sorry I upset him about the medicine,'' Gray said. ''He looked at me as if I was trying to feed him poison.''

''Don't take that too seriously,'' she answered. ''He was tired.''

''I've heard that excuse before.''

''It's making you tense,'' Jill realized aloud. Then added, almost too scared to say it because it seemed so ridiculous, ''And it's making you angry. Why, Gray?''

''Angry at myself.''

''Why? Not just that, I can tell.''

''Because I haven't earned his trust. I've tried, but it's not there.''

''You have. He was just—''

"Tired. Okay." He said it as if he didn't believe it. He was fobbing her off.

"But you're angry at him, too," she insisted.

"For not giving me a chance."

"He has. A dozen times. You're the one who doesn't give yourself a chance, Gray. Get it right, before you make accusations like that! Again, you're running your father's race. I—I wish to heaven you hadn't made me care so much about seeing you win. I'm so glad I'm leaving on Monday. *So glad!*"

Her voice threatened to break, but she managed to hold it together.

"Yeah, things will be simpler then, at least," he agreed. "For both of us."

There was a beat of silence.

It lasted long enough for Jill to be acutely conscious of Gray so near to her in the darkened hallway outside the room where Sam slept. Not wanting to waken him, or Pete, they had instinctively stood close together and they were keeping their voices low.

But every word they'd spoken was tense and strained, and every word cut another piece out of the clamoring heat of their physical connection. She wanted to ignore the problems, the widening gulf, and simply touch him. Wanted to pillow her head against his hard chest, feel the strength of him, kiss him the way they'd kissed before, in the yard, with all that heat and need and certainty.

She didn't need his next words to tell her it wasn't going to happen.

"It's late," he said. "I'd better let you get to sleep."

His voice was husky, now.

"Yes," she answered.

His whole body had changed, too, since she'd stood in his arms in the yard. It was stiff, distant, with his emotions bottled and tightly corked inside him. She didn't have to wonder about what had caused the change. He was worried about his mom. About how she'd react, in the long term, to this tangible new evidence about the extent of her estrangement from Mitchell. About how she'd feel if she couldn't see her new grandson. About the arguments she and Gray were bound to have, over and over, on the question of how to make it possible.

And all of this was set against the backdrop of their stretched finances, crushing workload, uncertain future and his unshakable belief that his father wouldn't have let any of it happen.

When I leave, Jill told herself, *Gray will barely notice. We'll be gone in a couple of days. He might think about us for a little bit...*

He would remember a joke he'd shared with her, maybe, and the times he'd read poems to Sam. She thought he would remember the way she felt in his arms, too, but that wouldn't last. It would fade.

But in a couple of weeks, all this, this time I've spent here, and everything he's made me feel, will be gone forever.

Chapter Nine

Gray took Louise, Jill and Sam to church the next morning.

Grandpa Pete decided he was going to give it a miss today. "My shoulder doesn't feel right. I'm going to take it easy."

The weather was still mild, but even Jill could tell it wasn't going to last. The temperature had begun to drop by the time they reached Blue Rock, and when they came out of the service of worship an hour later, some scattered flakes of snow were falling.

The house was silent when they reached home.

"Where is he?" Louise muttered. "If he's gone out in this…"

She didn't finish. She seemed pretty subdued and far away this morning, and Jill ached for her, could guess only too clearly what must be churning through her thoughts. On top of this, mother and son were barely speaking to each other. Probably because they knew they'd both let fly if they got started, and didn't want to do it in front of outsiders.

That's Sam and me.

"Dad?" Louise was calling, as she opened the back door.

No answer.

"I'll see if he's with the horses," Gray said.

He strode off to the old barn across the yard, and Jill had to fight to keep from watching him with naked hunger in her eyes. She loved his cowboy walk, loved the sense of purpose in it, and the way it claimed the ground beneath his feet as his own.

She followed Louise inside, starting to wonder about Sam's lunch, then heard the older woman let out a cry.

"Oh, I knew it! Oh, I knew I shouldn't have left him here! Here's a note, says he's gone for the cattle."

"What does that mean?" Jill asked stupidly.

"There's still a bunch of 'em up on the high pasture halfway up Blackjack Mountain. We hadn't had a chance to bring them closer in, ready for winter feeding. He's put the time on his note. Nine forty-five. That's only ten minutes after we left for church, and it's eleven-thirty now. He should have turned back when the snow hit, and he should be here by now. Jill, tell Gray—"

But Gray was back. "He's taken the four-wheeler," he said.

Jill knew that this was one of two small and almost new all-terrain vehicles, which many ranches used these days, when once they would have used horses.

"Why didn't he take Madie?" Gray went on. "At least she might have looked after him a little, if he'd gotten into trouble. He's always crazy on those four-wheelers. Tries to take 'em places you can only take a horse. He can't have thought the snow would come so fast. Mom, let's put something in our stomachs and then—"

"I can't." Louise pressed her hands to the tabletop and lowered herself into one of the old wooden kitchen chairs. Her voice was trembling and so were her legs.

"Can't eat?"

"Can't go. I want to. But I can't. I didn't sleep last night. I—just can't."

She was shaking so violently now that the table rattled beneath her hands. Then she snatched them quickly against the front of her lilac church blouse and Jill was afraid she was about to get sick to her stomach.

"Take some deep breaths, Louise," she urged. "I'll make you some—some hot chocolate." Something sweet, for quick energy. "Just stay right where you are."

Tears pricked behind her eyes and her throat ached. She'd gotten so fond of this kind, heroic woman. Didn't feel like she was a temporary and reluctant guest, soon to leave. Felt as if she and Sam both belonged, down to the last fiber of their souls.

"How about if I make some toasted sandwiches, or something, and we can eat quickly and then...then... Sam, honey, can you stay here and look after Louise? She's not feeling real well right now, and— Maybe you could find Firefly to curl up with her, and the two of you can look at stories while I go out with Gray to make sure Grandpa Pete's okay."

"Is he lost?" Sam asked in his sweet, innocent

voice. He was wide-eyed, and he'd caught the mood of fear.

"No, honey, he's not lost." We're praying he's not lost. "But he's trying to do a job with the cattle that's going to be too hard for him on his own in this weather, and we need to help."

We?

Well, she didn't know how much help she would be, but the idea of Gray going off alone after his grandfather appalled her. There was an intuition prickling like electricity in the room, and they all shared it. Something wasn't right. He should have turned back.

"That's right, Jill," Gray was saying. "Make some lunch. I'm going to saddle up Highboy, and you'll take the pickup as far as it can go."

"Says in his note he took the radio," Louise came in, still sounding weak and shaky.

After holding herself together for so many months, she'd now arrived at the edge of a complete emotional collapse, following the news about Mitch and her new grandson last night.

"I'll take the other one and start trying to reach him as soon as there's a chance of being in range," Gray said. "Here's hoping he *shows up* in the next ten minutes, and I can yell at him for this!"

But Pete didn't.

Jill piled together some toasted ham and cheese sandwiches, and settled Louise on the couch in the living room to eat them, with Sam and Firefly.

"I guess I must be getting sick," the older woman said, more than once. "A virus, or something."

She seemed bewildered by her own state of weak-

ness and emotion, and Jill hid in the kitchen for a minute or two and called Dr. Blankenship because she was
so worried.

"You know what? I'm going to stop by," the doctor
said in a decisive voice. "Visit with her a little, just in
case. You're right, Jill. This isn't like the Louise
McCall I know."

"She had some difficult news last night."

"Maybe it'll help her to talk it out a little."

"I think it might."

"I'll be there in about half an hour, okay?"

"Thanks, Doctor." Jill almost cried with relief.

Gray had the horse and the truck ready. He led the
way on Highboy, and Jill followed in the vehicle. She
felt in her shoulders, hands and jaw the same tension
she'd seen in Louise that day, more than a week ago,
when they'd gone on a picnic to fix fence. You couldn't
drive on a rough track like this, with snow coming
down faster and thicker every minute, and have any
thoughts left over for anything else.

Ahead, she saw Gray urging the horse forward, using
one hand on the reins as he held the two-way radio to
his ear with the other. From this distance, she couldn't
tell whether or not he was getting any response.

He wasn't, she found out a few minutes later.

They reached a gate and he swung down off Highboy to open it for the vehicle to go through. The animal
was a little skittish as Jill came past, making slushy
blue-gray tracks in the deepening snow. Gray controlled Highboy easily.

Rolling the window down a little, Jill asked him,
"Anything?"

"Static," he answered. "Either he's got it switched off, or—"

"How are we going to find him?"

"Pray that he's stuck to the obvious route. We'll hit a kind of a gulch just up ahead, and you're going to have to stop and come on with me."

"Come on with—? You mean, on the horse."

"Yup."

Her gaze fixed on his face and wouldn't move.

He added, "You're little. You'll fit. And Highboy is strong."

She nodded. "Uh…huh."

Her heart began to pound.

Suddenly, he grinned. The teasing light in his black eyes arrowed straight into her soul. "You mean I've at last found something on this ranch that you're *not* happy to tackle, Jill Brown?"

"You know I've never sat on a horse in my life. You know I'm a little…"

"Respectful of them?" he suggested.

It was a word she'd used herself a couple of times, but on this occasion, she had to admit to the truth. "Yes," she said. "Respectful spelled s-c-a-r-e-d."

He didn't answer, just went on boring that black-eyed gaze right through her for another five seconds, as if he was waiting. Very patiently. Full of understanding. For her to say…

"Let's do it, Gray. It's just a horse, isn't it? Not an elephant."

Jill drove behind him for another fifty yards, then he reined in the horse and they both stopped. She cut the engine then watched him try the radio one more time and shrug, his shoulders tight. She jumped out of the vehicle, pocketed the keys, grabbed the bag he'd packed with some emergency supplies and caught up to him.

He had stayed on the horse. He reached for the bag and fastened it to the saddle just in front of him. Jill stood beside the big animal, feeling its warmth in contrast to the snow that was feathering her jacket and hat. Both she and Gray were warmly dressed, but the cold was still a powerful force.

Gray reached down his hand, loosed his foot from the stirrup and said, "Stand close beside him. Get your foot in. Swing your leg over as soon as you're up. And just take it calm and steady. They gripped each other's wrists and he counted, "One, two, three, go!"

Highboy shifted, stamped his hooves, snorted some air through his big, loose lips, but Jill was safe and up where she should be, right behind Gray.

Absolutely *right* behind him. The insides of her thighs were pressed against the chaps he wore for warmth on top of his jeans. Her breasts squeezed into his broad back. Her hands found the big belt buckle at his waist and gripped it like she had gripped the steering wheel of the pickup. She could feel every movement he made, and she was swamped in the fresh, hardworking, outdoor smell of him that hypnotized her senses.

"Relax," he said.

"I am."

"If you say so."

He didn't waste any more time, just clicked his tongue and nudged with his heels and they were off at what she knew was walking pace, though it felt a whole lot faster. And rougher. Until gradually she did relax. Did his body have something to do with it? She could feel the rhythm, the unity of man and horse. His back sheltered her face and she didn't try to do anything clever, just sat, watched, listened, as best she could.

It wasn't long before they found him, hearing his call, first, through the falling snow.

"Gray, is that you?"

"Grandpa Pete? Where are you?" Gray veered a little, to follow the sound of the faint voice.

"In the gulch."

"We're coming."

He edged Highboy over the grass-tufted lip of ground and down into the eroded creek bed. It had become a small ravine, over time, about twenty feet deep, with raw, crumbling sides. They saw the old man straight away, a dark shape like an old coat flung on the steeply sloping ground. Jill could see that his leg was stuck out at a strange angle, and his face looked blue and muddy with cold.

"Darn four-wheeler," he said, as soon as he saw them. He tried to sit up on his elbow, but didn't have the strength. "Shoulda taken Madie, but I figured the four-wheeler would be quicker. Fool of an old man."

"What happened to the radio?" Gray had already dropped from the horse. He reached his hand up and Jill managed a clumsy dismount. Highboy wasn't impressed. He allowed himself to be tied to a handy branch, but it wouldn't have held him if he'd seriously considered making a bolt for home. He didn't seem very impressed by the snow in his face, either.

"Radio broke when the four-wheeler slid out from under me."

"Where *is* the four-wheeler, Grandpa?"

"Down there."

Pete gestured at the bottom of the ravine, where the small all-terrain vehicle lay on its back like a bug with its legs in the air, already thickly feathered with snow. Even from here, with her limited knowledge, Jill could tell it was badly damaged.

"Shoot!" Gray said.

"Yeah, shoot *me!*"

"You've broken your leg."

"Tell me something new, why doncha? Least the bone isn't actually sticking through the skin!"

"How in heck are we going to get you back?"

"Put me on the horse."

"It'll hurt like blazes, Grandpa Pete."

"I know. Hurts like blazes already, but I'm too cold to wait here while you bring in the emergency services."

"There's a blanket here, Pete," Jill said. She draped it over him, tried to tuck it closely around.

"Thanks, honey, but that isn't going to do much," the old man said. "I've been here an hour or more. Can't feel my fingers, or my feet. At my age, that's a heck of a lot more dangerous than the darned leg. We're just going to have to do this."

"Can you move your arms?"

"I haven't broken my spine, if that's what you mean. I'm just numb from the cold…"

"Okay, then."

"…and cursing myself for a fool."

"Never mind about that! Don't waste your strength."

Somehow, they managed to do it, but only because Pete's pain tolerance was honed from a lifetime of rugged physical labor, Jill suspected. He lay across the saddle with his leg dangling, and Gray had to shore him up with one shoulder to hold him in place.

"Can you untie Highboy and walk him on back to the vehicle, Jill?" Gray said. "I'm going to have to stay back here keeping Grandpa from falling off."

She nodded, swallowed her "respect" for the animal and took the supple leather of the reins in her gloved hand. Highboy seemed to know that this wasn't an occasion for playing games, or for testing the mettle of an inexperienced city girl. He walked steadily, and didn't need to be told to follow his own hoof prints back through the snow.

"Whisky or water, Grandpa?" Gray asked Pete. "I've brought both. And chocolate."

"Whisky," the old man said through gritted teeth, and a minute later Jill heard him splutter as the alcohol burned down his throat. He took several big gulps, treating it like a primitive kind of pain relief. Five minutes after that, he started singing.

"Grandpa, are you drunk?"

"No, just taking my mind of my danged leg."

"Here's the truck," Jill said.

"Hall-eee-luu-yah-and-glory-be!" Pete replied, which made her think he might be a little drunker than he admitted to.

He had a right to be! She couldn't even think about how much this had to be hurting, and the truck would be just as hard to bear. They got him as comfortable as they could, propped at an angle in the passenger seat, then Gray told her, "If you can follow the tracks home—they're not quite covered yet—I'll go ahead and tell Mom, call an ambulance."

"Dr. Blankenship should be there already," she remembered aloud.

"What?"

"I called her before we left. I was so worried about your mom, and the doctor said she'd drop by."

"Bless you, Jill," he said. "I mean that. Bless you from the bottom of my heart."

He gripped her shoulders, and the promise of a kiss hung in the air, as pure and glistening as the falling snow. But then he turned away and it didn't happen. He wasn't going to take the time. She understood that. She felt the same. They had to get Pete to the hospital.

Louise, Sam and Dr. Blankenship were waiting with Gray when Jill and Grandpa Pete slid to a halt in the yard. Louise was in tears, but oddly she seemed more in control than she had an hour earlier. She'd lost that look of totally sapped strength, and there was color in her cheeks.

"Dad," she sobbed. "Oh, Dad, *when* are you going to realize that you're seventy-eight years old?"

"When I'm about a hundred," he answered. He laughed, hiccuped, then gave a groan and a sob of pain as Gray and Dr. Blankenship carried him into the house.

They had hot fluids ready for him to drink, and the doctor had a morphine injection prepared for the pain. She rigged up a temporary splint for the leg, and a sling for the sprained shoulder he hadn't troubled to mention until now. She also dressed some shallow lacerations down his side. He hadn't thought to mention those before, either. His extremities had just begun to feel warm by the time the ambulance arrived, to take him to the hospital in Bozeman.

Louise began to say something about driving to town in its wake, but Dr. Blankenship pounced on her before the words were even out of her mouth.

"Yes, you're going to the hospital," she agreed. "But you're coming as a passenger in *my* car! Gray can pick you up this evening, after you've seen your dad settled in for the night."

Louise didn't argue.

As the ambulance set off down the road, watery sunshine began to break through the clouds, turning the snow into swirling diamonds.

"Phhfff!" Highboy blew through his lips and shifted his hooves once more.

"You did good, fella," Gray told him as he loosed the saddle girth and lifted the heavy piece of padded leather from the horse's back. "You didn't jolt Grandpa Pete, and you didn't spook Jill. You did good," he repeated.

He couldn't fill his praise with the firmness and sincerity he wanted. He felt as if his heart was being torn slowly into strips. A part of it was off in the ambulance with his grandfather, heading in to Bozeman, deeply thankful that the old man would live. And how about the cattle Grandpa had set out to bring down? They'd live, too. The storm was blowing over sooner than Gray had feared, and there was enough forest for them to shelter in, up on the higher slope of the Blackjack Mountain pasture.

Another part of his heart was with his mother, who had somehow dragged herself out of a nervous collapse by tugging a little harder, yet again, on her own bootstraps. Some TLC from little Sam and Barbara Blankenship had helped, but Mom had done most of it on her own.

She had hardened herself to the idea that she couldn't be spared from the ranch to see her new grandson, the same way she'd hardened herself to Mitch's leaving Montana all those years ago, and his not speaking to her or coming to Dad's funeral. It hurt, but she lived with it.

The good news was that she'd see little Cody a lot sooner than she thought, and get an important chance to mend fences with Mitch, though Gray wasn't going to tell her that yet. He should wait until he had set everything in motion before he told her that the time had come—no more ifs, no more buts—to sell the ranch.

What was that saying about "the straw that broke the camel's back?" This particular camel had been loaded up with two of those "last straws" in the past twenty-four hours. The first was Mom's feeling for baby Cody. The second was Grandpa's accident.

Time had come to look the truth full in the face. They couldn't keep going like this, stretched thinner and tighter than a piece of catgut on a homemade fiddle. If a fifty-four-year-old woman couldn't see her own grandson because she couldn't afford the time or the money to leave the ranch... If a seventy-eight year old man was mentally thrashing himself and calling himself a fool because he'd tried and failed to bring in some cattle in a snowstorm on a vehicle he didn't handle well at the best of times—and he'd wrecked the vehicle—*and* the radio—and they couldn't afford to replace either...

Oh, lord, yes! The time had well and truly come. Gray would call a Realtor in Bozeman first thing tomorrow and arrange to get Flaming Hills officially onto the market as soon as possible. Jill and Sam would be gone just hours before the signs went up along the section of fence that fronted County Route 18.

And when Jill and her son went, they'd take another strip of his heart along with them, and he would wonder for the rest of his life whether things might have been different.

Very different.

If they'd had more time. If there wasn't a practical man named Alan in Jill's life back east, who quite possibly understood what love and marriage meant a lot better than Gray himself did. And if Gray wasn't trying so hard—still trying, despite what Jill had said to him last night—to run his father's race.

He buried his face in Highboy's warm neck. The horse twitched, then craned to look back at him as if to say, "Hey, what's with you tonight? Where's the apples 'n' sugar 'n' stuff? I earned it, didn't I?"

"Yeah, you earned it," he told the horse, his voice harsh with weariness, and turned to the jar on the shelf behind him, where he kept the sugar.

Chapter Ten

Jill was packed by seven in the morning, apart from Sam's little pajamas, because he was still asleep and wearing them. Kneeling on the floor, she zipped their travel bag half shut, then looked up to find his eyes fixed on her. They were still owl-like from sleep, and his dark hair was rumpled.

"Our vacation's over," he said, as he took in the meaning of her action.

"That's a little sad, isn't it?"

"Can we come again soon?"

Oh, my!

"It's too far, honey."

"Maybe they could come stay with us, next time, at Cousin Pixie's?"

"Maybe they could," she agreed.

It wouldn't happen. Was she deceiving him, lying to him? Or was it one of those acceptable vaguenesses most people turned to, at times, with children? You could hurt them and disappoint them now, while it was fresh, yes. Or you could say things like "maybe" and "we'll see" and "one day," and hope they'd soon forget.

He will forget, she told herself. A lot quicker than I will. I can't kid myself with "maybe" and "one day."

She had hardly seen Gray since they'd returned with Pete through the snow yesterday afternoon. He'd been busy around the ranch until dark. After a gulped evening meal, he had driven straight down to Bozeman to visit his grandfather and bring Louise home. They had a good report on Pete's condition, but the break was a bad one, and as Dr. Blankenship had predicted, he would be in the hospital for a while.

Louise had immediately begun to plan, out loud, how they'd manage the work of the ranch while visiting Pete at the same time, but Gray had cut off the flow of words, his face tight with suffering.

"It doesn't matter anymore, Mom," he'd said, looking as if the words were killing something inside of him. "We can afford to hire on a couple of hands, now, to tide us over for as long as it takes. I didn't want to talk about this today...."

"What do you mean, we can afford?" Louise had asked blankly. "Why can we suddenly—?"

"We have to sell. And the bank will give us a bridging loan if the place is on the market."

"Gray—!"

"Please don't argue, Mom. You know it's true." From his face, it looked as though every word he spoke was cutting deep into his heart. "It was probably true last spring, or even before that, only we wouldn't let ourselves see it. Now it's screaming at us. I'm not going to stand by and watch you kill yourself, the way Grandpa Pete almost did today, because you won't give up the fight. And I'm not going to watch you deny yourself the chance of seeing your grandson and spending some time with Mitch. The ranch is up for sale.''

He had walked out of the kitchen before a shaken Louise could find the breath to answer him.

Now, even while she was packing Sam's pajamas, Jill felt a crazy urge to tell Gray and Louise that she was staying on here. To share this with them, the way she had shared so much else over the past two weeks.

She mocked herself.

What, stay on so you can help hammer in the ''For Sale'' signs, or something? They don't want you here. This is their private pain, and you don't share it. All they want is for you to get yourself and your child out of here as quickly and quietly as possible, so they can deal with what this means on their own.

When Sam was dressed, she brought him downstairs for breakfast. Outside, the sun was shining, and yesterday's short-lived snow was melting into thin, lacy patterns on the ground. Gray and Louise were out in the barn. Jill called Ron Thurrell and confirmed that she'd be arriving to pick up the rental car later that morning.

She fed Sam some cereal, toast and juice, heard the washing machine click off and put the laundry in the drier for Louise, cleared away the breakfast, cleaned the kitchen a little, and then heard Gray opening the back door.

''We're ready to go,'' she told him.

"I'll grab the keys. Mom's coming, too."

The twenty-minute drive into Blue Rock was soon over. Gray loaded Jill's travel bag straight into the trunk of the snappy little rental car waiting in Ron Thurrell's garage.

"Shouldn't have any trouble with this one," Mr. Thurrell said. "Now if we could just take care of the paperwork..."

He brought out a thin file from behind his cluttered desk in the back office of the garage. As before, Jill wasn't too impressed with his setup, despite his outward helpfulness. He had insurance papers mixed up with receipts for mechanical work, and three different business cards in a holder on his desk. "Thurrell Motor Repairs," read one. "Ron Thurrell, Licensed Agent, Triple Star Insurance," claimed a second. "Thurrell Car Rentals, affiliated nationwide." That one, at least, she could attest to.

"Sure," she answered Thurrell. He seemed sober today, in contrast to Saturday night at the Sheehans' ranch, when he'd raved at Gray and almost trampled Sam down.

"We'll wait outside, okay, Jill?" Gray said.

"Okay," she answered.

There was no real need for Gray and his mother to wait at all. They could each have said a quick goodbye, and it would have been over. Jill had the signed divorce papers in her bag. Last night, Alan had agreed over the phone to meet her and Sam in Chicago on Wednesday evening for a three-day vacation.

But she hadn't argued with Gray's suggestion that he and Louise wait outside.

I don't want to say goodbye.

Not yet. Put it off, even for just a few minutes longer.

"You had a good visit, there on the ranch," Mr. Thurrell said, in a tone of sly good humor. His words distracted her as she tried to fill in the details on the car rental form.

"A little longer than we planned," she agreed.

"Heading back east, now?"

"With a stop in Chicago."

"How're they doing, anyways, the McCalls?" Very casual.

"Oh, fine," she hedged, wondering if he had been too drunk to remember what he'd said the other night.

"Cuz you look a bit like a rat deserting a sinking ship. I heard old Pete's in the hospital. Hard to see how they'll manage now." He couldn't keep the satisfaction out of his voice.

"Oh, they'll manage!" The false brightness and confidence in her tone must have annoyed him, because the cheerful manner emitting from behind the desk was suddenly gone.

"Oh, come on, now!" he said impatiently. He was angry. "Don't give me that! How much longer can they string it out, the way they're stretched? They know me and my sister want to buy our family place back. Why won't they sell to us? If I'd a known they'd hang on this long without the capital—"

He broke off suddenly.

Jill felt a shiver of shock ripple down her spine. "What capital?"

"Without capital, I said."

"No, you said without *the* capital. Like it was a particular amount. You talked about capital the other night, too, at the cookout."

"No. You got it wrong, girlie," he growled. There was deliberate menace in his voice. As he leaned toward her, she saw sweat glistening on his jowls. "You've misunderstood."

"Have I?" She narrowed her eyes and watched his face, her skin pricking with intuition. Without looking down, she picked up one of his business cards and started flipping it over in her hand. It was a gesture that betrayed her own increasing uneasiness. She realized the fact, and laid the card down again on the desk at once, with a snap.

His gaze followed the sound, and hers dropped for a moment, too. She saw that it was one of the Triple Star Insurance cards. "You got it wrong," he repeated, his voice rising with each word.

"You said that Frank knew he needed capital to cover the costs of an expanded holding. You said—"

"We weren't stealing it." His gaze was locked with hers, and his greasy hand had shot across the desk to clamp hard around her wrist. "Stay out of this, okay?" He was almost shouting now. "You better realize that this isn't your concern or, believe me, you'll regret it."

Jill tried to twist her arm out of his grip, but she couldn't. He had strong fingers, and he was hurting her. She hardly noticed a darting movement at her side, and Ron didn't either. His light brown eyes were staring fiercely into hers.

"You'll regret it," he repeated on a growl.

"How?" Jill forced her voice into a yell. Sam had

disappeared out the side door. That was the movement she'd just seen from the corner of her eye. Had he gone to get help? Gray was waiting outside. He'd hear if she yelled loudly enough. He'd meet Sam halfway. "How, Mr. Thurrell? Just what exactly are you planning on doing to me?"

From outside the garage, waiting with his mother, Gray heard the sound of raised voices just moments after Sam appeared. He had shot out the side door like a racehorse out of a starting gate. His little face was white, but his legs were pumping so fast they were almost a blur, and he reached Gray in seconds.

"It's that man again," he yelled, dragging urgently on Gray's arm. "That man who hurt my ear at the cookout. This time, he's gonna hurt Mom, Gray, and this time he means it and you have to save her."

His lip began to tremble and he drew in a sharp, jerky breath.

"Honey…!" Louise said, and scooped him up in her arms.

Gray didn't wait. He charged for the garage. In the back of his mind, he had just a moment in which to think, *Sam came to me. When he needed help, he trusted me….* Then he had swung himself around the frame of the side door and cut Thurrell's grip on Jill's wrist with the twist of his arm and the sound of his voice.

"What the hell is this about?"

Jill didn't look too steady on her feet. She staggered against him and he whipped an arm around her shoulder, felt his stomach go queasy and heavy with need for her, and the muscles around his head tighten with anger.

"What the hell is this about, Thurrell?" he repeated.

"Gray, he—he said something about capital," Jill stammered. "The capital. Like there's some money. For you. A particular amount that he knows about." She picked up one of Ron's business cards and frowned at it. "Insurance," she said slowly. "Frank McCall's insurance. That's what it is, isn't it, Ron?"

"Dad didn't have any insurance with Triple Star. What the damned hell is this about, Thurrell?" Gray repeated for the third time, just as Louise entered through the office's main door.

The man collapsed like a limp balloon. "It's okay," he said, and buried his sweaty face in his sweaty hands. "I'm not a criminal. Me and my sister just wanted what should have been ours. This whole thing was a big mistake. We didn't think it'd take so long to break you. We thought you'd have given up months ago. I'll tell you. Take it easy, and I'll tell you all about it."

"Mr. Garrett, will you please explain this whole thing to me in words of one syllable or less!" Louise McCall said.

Her face was pale and as tired as a handkerchief that had been washed a thousand times, but there was a bright glitter of dawning hope in her dark eyes. It was late morning, and she and Gray, Jill and Sam were all sitting in the cozy private office of the McCalls' long-time lawyer, Haydon Garrett. He had spent the past hour sorting out the truth.

"Well, it's quite simple, really," the lawyer began,

then paused. "Well, no I guess it's not." He began again. "Bottom line is, your dad knew exactly what he was doing when he bought the Thurrell Creek ranch last December, Gray. Problem was, he didn't get a chance to explain it to you."

"I knew it," Louise murmured. "I knew there were things he wanted to say that last day in the hospital."

"Most definitely," Mr. Garrett agreed. "Once Stannard and your father and I had completed our work on the sale, Stannard dropped by Ron Thurrell's garage to tell him the news. Thurrell was furious that Stannard had sold to Frank and came looking for him."

"Looking for Dad..." Gray echoed.

"Found him in his car in Main Street, about to head home. They had an argument, which got so heated that it triggered your dad's stroke. Ron called the ambulance, as you know, then waited it out for a couple of days. When Frank died without regaining his speech, Ron was able to act. Or rather, he failed to act. He never told you about this."

Haydon Garrett pushed a thin manila file across the table, opened it up and watched Louise study it with the same helpless expression she had worn for quite some time.

"Life insurance," she said. "That's a huge policy, Haydon."

"Very generous, yes," the lawyer agreed.

"I never knew. That's not the company we use for the ranch's other insurance. Frank had a huge Whole Life insurance policy he paid into and never told me about in over thirty years! That's because of my eldest son. Anything involving money Frank always kept close to his chest.''

Again, the lawyer agreed. ''Extremely close. He never told me about it, either.''

''Because of Mitch. It got to be a habit after half a lifetime, I guess, but it started with Mitch. He didn't want Mitch to know. From the beginning, he never trusted my son.''

''No, Mom,'' Gray interjected. His voice was strained. ''It wasn't that way, was it? It was Mitch who never trusted Dad. Dad tried so hard to—''

''It cut both ways, Gray,'' she answered him, reluctance coloring her voice. ''But it began with Frank. That's hard for me to admit, but it's true. You never saw it. You weren't even born, at first. And then you loved your dad so much. And he was a good man. The best man. But he'd known Blaine, before Blaine and I married, and he never liked or trusted him. And from the beginning, he always saw Blaine's personality so strongly in Mitch. He tried, but he couldn't let that go. He couldn't trust Blaine's son. No wonder those two could never build a relationship.''

''It began with Dad...'' Gray echoed. ''I never understood that.''

His eyes were black and impossible to read. He seemed far away in thought.

''It was due to mature this past spring.'' Mr. Garrett turned back to the policy and pointed to a date printed on it. ''Frank knew that, of course, and knew it would have financed the costs involved in rebuilding Thurrell Creek and maintaining Flaming Hills.''

"But what did Ron and C.J. *want?*" Louise shook her head.

"Something which they almost got, Louise," the lawyer said. "To force you to sell Thurrell Creek to them. To pay you back for Frank beating them to it last December. We'll need to discuss with the police whether you're going to press charges, and you've got a lot of work ahead of you, sorting out how you need to allocate this money to get the expanded ranch back on its feet as soon as possible. But I guess right now you need a little time to think."

"I—I should go," Jill said. "It's past eleven, and Sam and I need to get to Trilby tonight."

The lawyer looked a little surprised, but then his face composed itself into a suitably bland expression. "Sure. The police may need to take a statement from you at some point, as to what transpired between yourself and Mr. Thurrell. Gray will have your contact details, of course."

"Yes, he has those."

There was an awkward scraping of chairs.

"I'm so happy about the ranch," Jill said to Louise. Her voice sounded all wrong.

She would have liked to say the words to Gray, but didn't trust herself with anything that came from her heart, just knew she would cry. It felt as if some vital organ was being torn from her body. Her unshed tears stung like acid and every muscle in her body was knotted.

"Thank you," Louise said.

"Let us know when you reach home," Gray added. Something in his mouth tasted like dust, and the words seemed to echo over and over in his mind, with less meaning every time. Was his whole body turning to fire and ash? Felt that way.

"I know." Jill nodded. It was a vigorous movement that suggested impatience to be on her way. "The statement for the police. I'll keep in touch."

Their eyes met, and Gray wondered if his looked as bloodshot and burning as they felt. Neither of them knew what to say or what to do. Maybe there wasn't any other possibility but this. Goodbye. So thin. Over so fast.

"I'll walk you out to the car."

"Don't." Sharp, as if she meant it.

"Okay…"

Less than a minute later, he heard the sound of the rental car's engine kick into life out front. It swelled and changed as she put her foot on the gas pedal, then faded as the car went down the street in the direction of Interstate 15.

How long before I can stop smiling? Jill wondered to herself. Her figure-hugging silver-gray dress felt stiff and tight and her matching shoes pinched. "Will Cattie and Patrick notice if I do?"

This is my sister's wedding, and I'm thrilled for her. She's just married a fabulous man, who looks at her as if the stars shine out of her eyes, the way Gray says his dad used to look at his mom….

The muscles in Jill's face ached in a way they would never have ached if her smile was genuine. Around her, wedding guests ate and danced and laughed. She was introduced to a dozen members of Patrick Callahan's huge family, and knew she wouldn't remember any of their names. Connor? Adam? Tom? Which was which? And which of these attractive women were their wives?

The large, formal rooms of this country mansion were gorgeously decorated. Several people were loudly staking their claim as fairy godmother to the newly married couple. Cat's cousin Pixie, garbed in fluffy lemon yellow, had her beau Clyde Hammond at her side in a shiny suit. Pixie and an old friend of Patrick's, Lauren van Shuyler, were both attempting to grab credit for the all-important and stunningly lovely dress.

Local councilman Earl Wainwright went much further than Lauren and Pixie, and insisted that there wouldn't have been a wedding at all if not for him. And it was true that Cat had only met Patrick in the first place because she'd gate-crashed a ball, Cinderella-style, back in June, in order to influence councilor Wainwright's vote.

"My idea," Jill said, remembering. "I was thinking a lot about Cinderella then...."

Thinking about her own Cinderella ball in Las Vegas in March, and how a handsome Montana cowboy had saved her from a wedding she didn't want. Strange. He'd done that twice, now. He'd saved her from a meaningless publicity stunt marriage to a drunken stranger, and he'd saved her, with all he'd taught her about love, from an even more disastrous marriage to Alan Jennings.

Things had fallen apart pretty fast in Chicago. They'd gotten back on Thursday, having cut their mini-vacation two days short. Not Alan's fault. No one's fault, probably.

He'd arranged for connecting rooms in a medium-priced hotel, and they'd gone out on Wednesday night for Chicago deep-dish pizza. By nine in the evening, Sam was asleep, the connecting door between the rooms was open and anything could have happened. Something *should* have happened. Alan had ordered flowers, candles, room service dessert and coffee. He'd bought her a ring.

"But I don't even need to get it out of the box, do I?" he had said, studying her across the candlelit table with his blue eyes.

"No, best not," she said. "You'll…have to return it, Alan."

"What happened out there? The magic didn't go away, did it?"

"No…"

"So how come you didn't stay?"

"Magic doesn't always work, I guess. Magic isn't enough."

Intuition, Gray had called it. Love starts with intuition and grows slowly, like moss growing on a tree. But there hadn't been a chance for that. Too many things in the way.

"No, it's not enough," Alan agreed. "My wife and I started with magic and managed to build a partnership on top of that. We were lucky. I—I still grieve for that. With you, I thought it might work the other way around. We'd start with the partnership and find the magic later."

"It's not going to happen, Alan."

"I can see that. You know, maybe at a whole lot of

levels, in any case, I'm still grieving too much about
Maureen…''

By mutual agreement, they'd closed the connecting
door, slept on opposite sides of it and checked out the
next morning. It had brought Jill home in time to help
prepare for Cat's short-notice wedding, but right now
she felt as if she might have preferred to miss the event
altogether. The final couple left in the Cinderella Marriage Marathon had claimed their prize last night on
live television. Interviewed afterward, they announced
their plan to file immediately for divorce.

All in all, Jill felt that she had had enough of wed-
dings.

Here was Cat now, with a big hug, her blond hair
like a golden halo, her cheeks pink, her eyes spar-
kling…and her lower lip getting chewed to pieces.

''She's noticed the smile,'' Jill decided. ''That's
why she's worried.''

She pasted it on even wider and even shallower.
Then she dropped it immediately, distracted, when Cat
blurted out, ''Jill, I hope I've done the right thing.''

Jill grabbed Cat's nervous hands. ''Oh, you have,
Cattie! Patrick's a—''

''Not that! Of course *that's* right.'' Her cheeks got
even pinker and her lips curved into a smile that just
wouldn't go away. ''But there was a phone call for you
this morning—well, *asking* about you—and I told
him—and the thing is, he's—''

Cat looked back over her shoulder across the
crowded room to the front entrance. She stepped back.
She gestured feebly.

''Jill, he's here.''

Grayson. Grayson James McCall.

"Gray..." she whispered.

He stood uncertainly, dressed in a dark suit. His cowboy hat was nowhere in sight. Then he caught sight of Jill, and his uncertainty disappeared like cattle-yard mud washing off in a strong, hot shower. She went toward him on legs that moved like wooden pegs. The crowd began to part, and when they reached each other, they could feel the curious heat of at least a dozen pairs of eyes.

He wasn't having that. Dragging her by the hand, he led the way out front, to the white-pillared portico, and leaned against it as if it were the trunk of a huge Montana tree. He pulled her close, and she sank into his arms wishing she'd never have to let go.

"That stuff I said about love, back home..." he began.

"Was so true, Gray," she cut in. "I've thought so much about it. I'm not going to marry—"

"...was so much bull-crud, okay? When it's right, it doesn't grow slowly. It— Hell, it explodes right in your face. And you can't think, and you can't work, and you can't—" He broke off, swallowed, looked down as if he expected to find a cowboy hat in his hands, ready to be crushed into shape and put back on his head. His hat wasn't there. He looked up again. "I told your sister on the phone that I was coming. She told me you'd be here. Here at her wedding, which seemed— I *love* you, Jill. I want to marry you."

"But, Gray, we're—"

"Heck, I know we're married already." His shoulders twisted in frustration. "I know that! But the first

time it didn't mean what it should have meant. I want
to do it again, say it all again, and mean it with my
heart this time, and I don't want to wait. I want you
back. I want Sam. He trusts me, and I care about him.
Mom wants you, too. She couldn't believe I let you
go. You fit in my life, Jill. You were great on the ranch.
Both of you.''

"I love the ranch, and your mom, and—"

"I'm *not* running my dad's race anymore, and I
know we can make it work. You got married to me
legally in March in a borrowed dress. Could you borrow a different dress and marry me again tonight, from
the heart this time?''

He didn't wait for her answer. Maybe he thought he
hadn't convinced her yet, and was prepared to work a
little harder on the problem. His mouth crushed against
hers, and his fingers splayed apart and raked along her
jaw. His fingers were trembling.

Jill could hardly draw breath. Didn't know if that
was because of Gray's mouth, or because she was crying. Crying with happiness, disbelief and wonder.
Here. He was here, and—

"F-from Cat?'' she stammered. Kissed him hungrily,
then pulled away. "Borrow the dress from Cat?''
Kissed him again. "Oh, yes! I love you… *Yes*, Gray.''

So the van Shuyler family mansion, in Mercer
county, New Jersey, staged a second wedding ceremony that night. Lauren van Shuyler had lent the dress
to Cat. Now Cat put on her honeymoon clothes and
lent Lauren's gown to Jill, who married her Montana
cowboy for the second time.

"Second and last?'' he said to her later, back at

Pixie's house. Sam was asleep but Jill and Gray weren't planning to get to that part of their schedule for quite a while.

"Except I kind of wish your mom and Grandpa Pete could have been here, too," she answered him. "Not that I'm sorry we did it. I didn't want to wait a second longer."

"Grandpa's still in hospital. As soon as he's home, Mom's going to Las Vegas to see Mitch and Lena and baby Cody. Lena called again a couple of days ago and announced their engagement."

"It would have been nice to have them here tonight, too."

"Then I guess maybe we'd better get you another dress and do it a third time back home at the ranch."

"Back home at the ranch," she echoed. "That sounds so good."

"Whenever you like. Your sisters can come out for a visit."

"It could get to be a habit, marrying you...."

"Why not? You look so good in a wedding dress. I thought that the very first time I saw you."

"Did you, cowboy?"

"So good, darlin'. So good..."

She kissed him, long and soft and slow, and he kissed her back. And, like the very first night they met, they didn't sleep until after dawn.

* * * * *

CALL THE ONES YOU LOVE OVER THE HOLIDAYS!

Save $25 off future book purchases when you buy any four Harlequin® or Silhouette® books in October, November and December 2001,

PLUS

receive a phone card good for 15 minutes of long-distance calls to anyone you want in North America!

WHAT AN INCREDIBLE DEAL!

Just fill out this form and attach 4 proofs of purchase (cash register receipts) from October, November and December 2001 books, and Harlequin Books will send you a coupon booklet worth a total savings of $25 off future purchases of Harlequin® and Silhouette® books, AND a 15-minute phone card to call the ones you love, anywhere in North America.

Please send this form, along with your cash register receipts as proofs of purchase, to:
In the USA: Harlequin Books, P.O. Box 9057, Buffalo, NY 14269-9057
In Canada: Harlequin Books, P.O. Box 622, Fort Erie, Ontario L2A 5X3
Cash register receipts must be dated no later than December 31, 2001.
Limit of 1 coupon booklet and phone card per household.
Please allow 4-6 weeks for delivery.

I accept your offer! Please send me my coupon booklet and a 15-minute phone card:

Name: _____

Address: _____ City: _____

State/Prov.: _____ Zip/Postal Code: _____

Account Number (if available): _____

---

097 KJB DAGL
PHQ4012

Celebrate the season with

Midnight Clear

A holiday anthology featuring
a classic Christmas story from
New York Times bestselling author

Debbie Macomber

Plus a brand-new *Morgan's Mercenaries* story
from *USA Today* bestselling author

Lindsay McKenna

And a brand-new *Twins on the Doorstep* story
from national bestselling author

Stella Bagwell

Available at your favorite retail outlets in November 2001!

Silhouette®

Where love comes alive™

Visit Silhouette at www.eHarlequin.com

PSMC